NOTES ON THE MOON PEOPLE

ALSO BY LINDA JORDAN

Falling Into Flight

Continental Divide

Living in the Lower Chakras

Bibi's Bargain Boutique

Horticultural Homicide

Poison Passion

Faerie Unraveled: The Bones of the Earth Series, Book 1

Rescue Mission: Islands of Seattle, Book 1

Come on over to Linda's website and join the fun!
www.LindaJordan.net

Don't miss a release!

Sign up for Linda's Serendipitous Newsletter while
you're there

NOTES ON THE MOON PEOPLE

LINDA JORDAN

METAMORPHOSIS PRESS

Published by Metamorphosis Press

www.MetamorphosisPress.com

ISBN:-13: 978-0997797183

For Michael & Zoe

CHAPTER 1 - PENELOPE

THE PROBLEMS BEGAN BECAUSE SHE WAS INVISIBLE.

Her long silver gray hair pulled back and fastened in a bun at the nape of the neck. She was stooped beyond her years, hunched over in an attempt to remain unseen and ignored by the world. She dressed in soft baggy jeans and even baggier pale colored T-shirts. And gray running shoes, although she never ran.

Penelope Mason had no desire to draw attention to herself.

Her whole life had been an attempt to become invisible. From her childhood filled with fighting parents, who spent years telling her in great detail every single thing that was wrong with her, to her friendless adolescence filled with books of all sorts, to her adulthood of lonely solitude.

Her only social interactions were when coworkers at the library brought her more books to repair. Penelope spent her time alone.

She never talked to anyone on the crowded bus; which always smelled like people who hadn't bathed in a month. Her face was always hidden in a book. For protection. She wore earbuds in her ears with the plug-in end tucked down in her coat, nothing attached to it.

She didn't mind silence.

People always hurt her.

She rode the bus home to her tiny studio apartment. It was furnished with a lumpy twin bed, an old overstuffed chair and bookcases made of concrete blocks and boards. The only view looked out on an alley. Penelope cooked meager meals for herself. She didn't deserve any better.

Penelope had no friends and her parents were, thankfully, long dead. Her life, one of routine and order felt meaningless.

She didn't do anything of any importance. Since she had few hopes or dreams, it felt unlikely that she'd ever do anything important either.

She didn't speak up for herself. She felt unhappy with her life, but unable to change it.

It was a Monday that it happened.

She'd been in the middle of her second cup of strong black tea when her boss, Janice, called Penelope into her office. The whole thing was blurred now. Something about the district needing to cut hours. She needed to work faster, to prove her worth. She was in competition with the only other book conservator in the district. One of them would be laid off in three months, at the end of the year.

Just after Christmas. Which she hated anyway.

Penelope left work with a sinking feeling in her belly. She'd be the one cut. She knew it. And there weren't many jobs like hers left. She'd have to move to a new city. Find a new job.

Or take early retirement. She probably didn't have that much saved.

She worried about it all the way on the cold bus ride home. She barely noticed the unwashed smelly man next to her.

Penelope couldn't concentrate on her book as her future

unraveled before her. She read the same paragraph countless times and remembered none of it.

The bus crept closer and closer to home. Her sanctuary. Rain dripped down the outside of the windows. Inside, the windows were fogged over, forming a barrier that obscured the coming darkness outside. At least she'd worn her raincoat.

It seemed to take forever to get home. Finally, it was her stop. She stuffed her book inside the forest green backpack, shouldered it, stood and walked out the door and down the steps onto the sidewalk. The bus drove off.

Except that this wasn't her stop.

Penelope looked back at the bus, to see if she'd taken the wrong bus number, but it was gone. The entire street was gone. There weren't any cars around, or sidewalks.

It was dark, nighttime, not rainy dark.

Confused she looked around and saw nothing but tall evergreen trees surrounding a grassy meadow.

The only thing that was constant was the rain. Dribbling down from the sky. She put her hood up and felt the water soaking into her running shoes.

The air smelled different, though. Stronger. Earthier and almost moldy.

Where was she and how had she gotten here?

She must have fallen asleep. This must be a dream.

A large furry dark shape moved towards her. She wasn't afraid of it. It looked quite friendly, almost like a huge green teddy bear. Sweet, kind eyes that seemed to cry out for love.

She felt more calm the longer she looked at it. It walked upright on two legs and must have been about eight feet tall. It was only a few yards from her when a squawk from a nearby tree got her attention.

She saw a dark form the size of her head, stretch its wings as if to shake off the rain.

Then the bird dive bombed her.

"Don't just stand there," it shrieked. "Run, follow," it said, turning its head to point the beak off to her right.

She turned to look.

Shadows ran through the darkness. People. Running. Then they stopped. Looking around. Some carried long sticks that looked like spears.

Penelope froze. Confused.

Maybe they wouldn't see her. Fear built in her belly.

The green bear-like thing was still moving slowly towards her.

Tension filled her muscles.

She couldn't run, like the huge black bird suggested, let alone follow. Follow what? She looked back at the bird. A raven? But it was gone. Ravens were very smart birds, but that didn't mean she should take its advice.

She closed her eyes, pretending she wasn't there.

I don't exist, she told herself.

"Who are you?" said a deep voice, grabbing her hand and pulling her along.

"No one," she whispered.

"You are someone. Come with us. The dawn is being born. It isn't safe," said the woman's voice. She continued pulling Penelope along and looking warily back at the green creature.

Penelope opened her eyes. Before her stood a woman. The woman was dressed in leather clothes, but Penelope couldn't see much detail. Dark hair and dark eyes, but the eyes looked larger than normal.

On the horizon a lightness appeared in the sky. The rain was lessening. The green creature was still slowly coming towards her.

"Come. You must get away from the hurracha. And *they* will be out soon."

"Who?" asked Penelope.

"The Day People. Run."

The woman ran and Penelope followed. Although she couldn't say why.

Shouting came from behind them. She heard a whirring sound and saw an arrow hit a tree beside her. She ran faster.

Penelope followed the woman into the trees, bushes slapping her in the face. She panted and tried to catch up. Felt confused.

Where was she? Her part of Seattle had no hills? This couldn't be Seattle. But it didn't feel like a dream either.

She struggled to get a breath. Out of shape.

The woman appeared in front of her. Penelope gasped, startled.

"This way," the woman said, turning down a path around a stone outcropping.

The trees had been so tall, Penelope hadn't even seen the mountain towering above them.

She ran, following the woman around the columns of stone and into a dark hole in the side of the mountain. Penelope slowed down, trying to breathe. She wasn't used to running at all.

The woman said, "Come," and Penelope followed her through a labyrinth of tunnels, narrow and short. Then they widened into large hallways and caverns. The stones glowed like backlit quartz, forming a dim light for her to see.

Up ahead, Penelope could see nine or ten people moving down the corridor. Some tall, some short, all carrying bulky loads. The tunnel smelled stuffy. People were sweating. But it smelled different than the people with her on the bus. Somehow, these people smelled clean.

Smoke wafted past her nose and the smell of cooked meat, like some of the restaurants she passed by on the way home from the bus. Her stomach growled and she remembered the tasty left over sausage and biscuits with gravy she'd planned for dinner tonight.

Why was she here and how had she gotten here and where was here anyway?

She followed the others into a large cavern, the size of a cathedral.

She stood gaping at the height of the ceiling and the complex woven tapestries on the walls. Two large fires burned on one side of the room, the smoke spiraling upwards to an opening high in the ceiling. The smoke moved quickly as if being sucked out there. Did it vent to the outside of the mountain?

Tables and benches made from carved logs lined the room and in the center was an open space where the people dropped their burdens.

Two bloody carcasses of large animals lay there along with a couple of huge bags, three large pottery urns and what looked like a pile of clothes.

"Aah, what did you find tonight?" asked an old man, who rose from a chair and peered into the bags. His voice echoed off the smooth cavern walls.

Penelope fingered a long welt on her cheek from where one of the bushes had slapped her. It still stung.

She stood towards the back of the others, trying to remain unseen. Strands of her long gray hair hung loose from her bun and she tried to push it back in. Her raincoat dripped water with quiet splats onto the stone floor.

Where should she go? How could she get out of here, wherever here was? No, she wasn't really here.

This must be a dream. No, a nightmare. She'd fallen asleep on the bus on the way home from work. It was about getting threatened regarding the lay off. She just wanted to be at home in her tiny apartment.

Alone.

She closed her eyes and said to herself, 'Please, please send me back home.'

"Ah, what have we here?" asked the old man.

She opened her eyes.

Everyone had stepped away from her, leaving her exposed. And more people were coming into the cavern.

He stood in front of her. She could almost feel his breath on her face. Her insides quivered, her face warmed. She knew it was red. She could barely keep herself from shaking. She kept looking at the floor. At her soaking wet shoes.

"You are not one of the Day People. Nor Moon People either. Where are you from?" he asked her.

She didn't know what to say. So for a long time Penelope said nothing. Finally, the silence was deafening and she whispered, "Another world."

Everyone laughed.

At her.

"No, only the hurracha come from another world. Surely you are not from that world."

"I don't know what a hurracha is," she whispered. "But I'm not from this world."

"A hurracha is a huge green furry beast. They stalk their prey in the woodlands, trapping it by speaking to the creatures' minds, making their prey stand still and not run away. They are fearsome predators and are out both day and night. It is well you came in with our raiders. The hurracha often prey on those traveling alone."

She shivered.

The teddy bear thing had been trying to kill her!

"You do not wear the clothes of our world, so perhaps what

you say is true. Perhaps you will stay with us and tell us of your world," he said, smiling at her.

Penelope's face still felt hot and it wasn't from the exertion, although she still was out of breath. She knew her face was tomato soup red. She kept looking down at her shoes as if they had a magical power to save her.

The man walked back towards the urns.

"Well, this is a good haul," the man said. "It has been a long time since we had barley and oats. And fresh beans. Aguila and Mabe, will you take the food to the kitchen? The rest of you help me sort through the clothing so it can be shared with those who need it."

Penelope backed up until she stood against the wall of the cavern. She watched them sort through the piles of clothes. The people seemed to be organizing them by size. Mostly they held up tunic looking clothes.

She felt hot in her raincoat and wanted to take it off, but she kept hoping that any minute now she'd wake and find herself at home in bed. And that this entire day would have been a bad dream. And she didn't want to leave anything behind in this dream world. She didn't want to have to come back for it. Or be tied to it.

She just wasn't the adventurous type.

One of the women who had been helping to sort clothes, came over towards her with an armload of clothes.

"If you don't change into some cooler clothes, you'll be roasted and we'll have to serve you for dinner."

Was she serious or joking?

The woman smiled and said, "Follow me and I'll take you to a place to sleep and change. Are you hungry?"

Penelope would have had dinner long before now, but she felt so upset by everything that any appetite had vanished.

"I don't know. I don't think so."

"Dinner won't be ready for a while yet. They are just beginning to set things up."

She followed the woman down corridors much smaller than the entrance to the big cavern. Some were smooth, others rough, like they'd been chiseled out. The stone colors changed. Slate gray to brown to whitish gray.

In places the tunnels were lit by stones that glowed. Other places, there were burning bowls set into holes in the walls. What were they burning? Animal fat or seed oils?

How would she ever get out of here? But did she want to if predators like the hurracha were out in the forest. She felt thoroughly lost.

The deeper into the mountain they went, the more earthy the smell. It didn't get any cooler though. Was the mountain volcanic? If so, it might erupt at any time.

"I'm Mala."

She didn't want to tell anyone her real name. Didn't want anyone to get close to her.

"I'm Hypatia," she said, then instantly regretted it.

She'd been reading too much Mediterranean History lately. And did she actually think she was good enough to name herself after a famous philosopher and mathematician? She, who had never accomplished anything in her entire life.

"What a beautiful name," said Mala. Her dark eyes flashed in the dim light.

They passed many people in the tunnels, some in groups, others walking singly. There weren't many as old as she was. But perhaps their hair didn't gray as much when they aged.

The old man in the big cavern had hair that was almost white. Her's was still a silvery gray. Her grandmother had had white hair.

Mala took her into a small cavern. She grabbed a handful of

glowing rocks from a crevice in the hallway and brought them in.

"This looks empty. I'll see that some rushes and sleeping furs are brought in. You can leave your clothes here and change into these," Mala said, handing her the pile of clothes.

Penelope took the clothes and just stood there, waiting for Mala to leave. But Mala was inspecting a stone shelf, which was apparently the bed. She blew on it raising a cloud of dust.

Penelope laid the clothes on another shelf and took off her backpack, setting it on an empty shelf. She unsnapped and removed her raincoat. Her T-shirt was soaking wet from sweat. She wished she could get a shower, but that was unlikely. She sat down on the shelf and took her wet running shoes off, without looking at the dust where she sat or whatever else might be on the floor. Better not to know.

She didn't think there was anything that could be done about it.

She slipped off her wet socks and set them aside. They would be going back on. She noticed Mala wore leather boots as had the others. Stitched like moccasins, except ending at the top of the calves, right below the knee. More practical for being outdoors in the wet. Although they looked damp from the darkness of the leather.

Penelope looked at the clothes and chose a periwinkle blue tunic. It would be too short, mid-thigh but was about the most modest of what she'd been given. She hadn't worn anything that showed that much skin since she was six probably. Maybe not even then.

"Is something wrong?" asked Mala.

"Where I come from, this is immodest."

"What does that mean?" asked Mala, a confused look on her face.

"We wouldn't wear something that shows so much of our skin."

"Are your people ashamed of your skin?"

"I, I don't know how to explain." She pulled off her T-shirt and laid it on the shelf, stretching it out to dry. Her bra was soaking wet. She supposed that would have to come off too or it would get the tunic all wet. She removed it and quickly slid the tunic on.

The fabric felt like soft cotton, soothing to her overheated skin. She stood and decided it was still too hot to wear her jeans and they were wet up to the knees from running through the brush. She unsnapped them and slid them off, feeling naked, even though she wasn't. And she wasn't removing her panties, at least they were partly dry. She drew the line at going commando.

She sat down and was about to put her wet shoes back on when Mala said, "Oh here, take these, they're dry." She pulled out from beneath the pile of clothes a pair of boots like she was wearing. Penelope hadn't seen them.

Penelope took the boots and slid them on. They fit perfectly. She tied them at the ankle and the top. And stood up.

"Okay?" she asked Mala.

The woman, chewed on her lip as if thinking while staring at her. Then she came closer and pulled the comb out that held Penelope's bun in place.

Her hair fell down to the middle of her back and felt completely out of control. She only wore her hair down when she was brushing it.

Mala fluffed it up, separating the strands with her fingers, stood back and said, "There you look perfect. Formidable."

Penelope didn't want to look formidable. She certainly didn't feel that way.

"Come Hypatia, the cooks will be serving dinner. You don't

want to miss it. The hunters brought in a boar and it's been cooking for two nights and days. I can almost taste it, juicy and tender."

Penelope followed her out into the passageway. She cast one look back longingly at her belongings, but she'd be back. Mala said she'd see that rushes and sleeping furs were brought in. She couldn't believe it would get cold enough here to need furs to sleep under. Maybe they were just to sleep on.

They ended up back in the large cavern filled with wooden tables and benches. And people. Penelope would never have imagined that many people lived beneath the mountain. She really hoped it wasn't a volcano. How could one tell?

Mala led her to a line where people took a wooden plate and dished up their own food. She pointed out the various types.

"Keena root, very good for you. And this is the roast boar. And chicken. We got some of the Day Peoples' chickens yesterday. And cooked greens, harvested from the forest."

Penelope dished up a bit of each of the unknown foods and followed Mala to a table. The smoky smells of the chicken and boar made her stomach rumble with hunger. She sat down next to Mala and began eating, ignoring the stares of the other people who were already eating.

She hesitantly scooped up some of the cooked greens with her wooden spoon and tasted them with her tongue. They were bitter and as she ate them, she noticed small chunks of meat cooked with them, which somehow made the greens taste better.

Penelope had never paid much attention to cooking.

Her skills included making salads and soups. And spaghetti. But mostly she bought prepackaged foods to eat. The sausage, biscuits and gravy had been leftover takeout food. It was too much trouble to cook for one person after a day at work. And she hardly ever ate in restaurants. it always felt embarrassing to eat alone in public. Yet she wouldn't have wanted company either.

Here, everything felt different.

She felt included somehow.

Mala indicated a large bowl of water and a towel. Penelope felt embarrassed that she hadn't even thought to use it. She washed her hands and dried them in the communal bowl.

How did they eat the meat, without a fork and knife? She watched Mala who picked up the pieces of chicken and just ate it.

Penelope shook her head at the barbarity of it, but did the same. The chicken tasted of smoke and herbs and melted between her fingers. It was luscious.

She'd never tasted anything so wonderful.

Until she bit down on some of the wild boar. Succulent and cooked with dried fruit and herbs, the flavors unraveled in her mouth. She ate until she felt stuffed. She wanted to eat more, it was so good, but didn't think any more food would fit in her stomach.

Two people were walking around filling wooden cups. Penelope sniffed at the cup.

"It's sinna wine. The golden sinna flowers grow in the meadows surrounding the mountain. We harvest them and make wine. We only have it for a short time, before it runs out, so enjoy," said Mala.

She didn't drink alcohol. She never had. Her parents used to drink a lot. And it only made them meaner than they normally were, but she was so thirsty, she had a sip. The wine tasted sweet and tangy at the same time. She had a few more sips. Then realized how exhausted she felt.

Mala finished hers quickly.

"I must go find my partner and children," she said.

"I don't think I can find my way back to where I need to sleep," said Penelope.

"I will take you, if you've finished your wine."

"I shouldn't have any more. I'm not used to it."

"Come, I'll take you to the stream. We can clean up before sleeping."

Mala took her down through another set of tunnels. The only way she knew it was different was that above the fire bowls blue wavy symbols were drawn. Penelope guessed they indicated water.

Then she heard the roaring sound.

They entered into a huge cavern through which a river rushed.

There was a long gash in the rocks off to the side. It was dug deep. Mala straddled it and pulled her tunic up and urinated. Then she took a pitcher of water and washed the urine away so it ran off into the river.

There was another place slightly upstream, where the water pooled. People waded in to bathe. Mala did the same, stripping off her boots and tunic. Under which she obviously wore nothing.

"Come," Mala said. "The water will help cool you before sleeping."

Penelope saw no way out of this. And she did need to pee.

She slipped out of her panties, crumpling them up in her hand to hide them. No way to do this with them on. She copied what Mala did, peed and shook herself off, then used the pitcher of cool water and refilled it.

Then she looked around, but no one was paying any attention to her. Pulling off her boots, she set them beside a rock. Slipped off her tunic and put it and the panties down on the rock and waded into the pool.

The stones beneath her feet felt smooth and cool as did the

water, but it wasn't cold. She walked quickly towards a deeper area so her body was covered by the water. And she bathed, scrubbing at her skin with her hands. And rinsing her hair again and again.

Everyone seemed in their own world. The only people talking were a woman and child.

"Momma, tell me why we have to bathe again," the little girl said.

"We bathe because we are alive. We come from water and water is what gives us life."

"I know that. But tell me the story of snake again."

"Well long ago, there was a snake who loved the dirt. The earth. She burrowed deeply and only came out to find food. She couldn't catch mice scampering through their burrows, but up on the surface she hid behind rocks and logs and caught them. But then, she began to stink. She never bathed."

"Not ever?"

"Never. And then the mice could smell her coming. They ran away, holding their noses she smelled so bad. She was starving. And that was when raven saw her.

He said, 'You'll never catch any food smelling like that. You need to go into the river and clean yourself off.'

'But I'm afraid I'll drown,' she said.

'I'll show you how to be safe,' he said.

She followed him into a small eddy at the side of the stream. He stood on a rock, so the water was only as deep as his knees and he wet his wings and bathed. She slid onto another rock and rolled around in the shallow water, not drowning.

'This feels wonderful,' she said.

The water revived snake, who had been almost dying. She drank some of it and the water rolled around in her empty belly. She was so hungry and then she got an idea. She lunged at raven, who flew up into a tree and just laughed at her.

He was much too big to eat anyway.

She left the river and went back to hunting mice again, who couldn't smell her coming now. And that's the story of snake," the woman said.

"I like that story," said the little girl.

"I do too. Now finish rinsing off your hair. It's time to sleep. The sun has been up for a long while."

Penelope looked down and noticed swirls of luminescence flowing through the water. Green, pink, melon and blue patterns formed and vanished. The shapes reminded her of the marbled endpapers from some of the older books she repaired, except a hundred times more vivid and all different colors. And alive.

"The tuallia are swimming!" said a man, excitedly.

Everyone began laughing and swirling their hands in the water.

"What are tuallia?" asked Penelope, finally getting up the nerve. Her curiosity winning over the insecurity.

"Tuallia are tiny colorful creatures that live in the water. When the world gets warm enough and they begin to swim, that's our signal summer is coming. That's when we move to our summer home."

Penelope nodded.

Mala left the water and Penelope followed her. The woman picked up her clothes and began to walk towards the tunnel, naked.

Penelope tried to do the same. There wasn't time to dress, she didn't want to lose Mala, and not be able to find the way back to her cave.

The rocks here were sharper and hurt her feet. She walked gingerly, losing ground.

"Mala wait. My feet aren't as tough as yours."

Mala turned towards her and waited.

She felt like the child in the pool. Everything was new to her and she felt like a beginner at everything. That child was young and still learning and growing. She was old and still learning. But she was finished growing.

Or was she? Was it possible that she could continue to grow?

Those around her wouldn't be patient enough to wait for her though. Not on Earth or not here, wherever she was.

When she'd caught up to Mala, she said, "Maybe I should put my boots on."

"Then your feet will never get hard. Better to leave the boots off until you can't stand it anymore, then put them on to give your feet a little rest. When your feet are rested again, remove the boots. We only wear boots when we go outside. The day people set cruel traps for us that cut our feet and legs.The boots help us survive. Mostly."

Mala led her back to the her cave, her room.

The floor had been covered with the stalks of soft green grasslike plants, they must be the rushes. They gave off a fresh and clean smell.

And there was a pile of furs laid on one of the shelves. Her clothes lay dried and stiff on the other shelf, along with her backpack.

"I will come get you when it is time to wake, or I will send someone else, if I can't come."

"Thank you," said Penelope. "I wish I wasn't such trouble."

"You are no trouble," said Mala, coming and grasping both her hands. "It is an honor to help you. I am simply worried about my son. He fell and hurt his arm yesterday. My partner is with him but I know he is in pain."

"Oh, you should be with him. Don't worry about me."

"I do not worry. You will be fine, but you still need a guide through our home. There are many caverns which would take you so deep into the mountain you would never be found. So, until you can find your way, someone will be with you. I am honored to be that person," she said, laying her hands above her own heart. "Sleep well."

"Thank you and you as well. I hope your son is feeling better."

"Thank you. He will be thrilled that you thought of him and you never having seen him."

Mala disappeared into the darkness.

Penelope stood there naked, wondering what to do. She folded her stiff jeans and T-shirt. Then bundled up her dried socks. She put all these into her nearly empty backpack. All she had in it were her apartment keys, her wallet, some chapstick and a copy of the the current bestseller she was reading. Oh, and a couple of kleenex. No chocolate or tea or anything that might be valuable here.

She set her running shoes on the ledge by her backpack. Then laid out her tunic on the ledge as well. She didn't want to get it dirty. Who know when she could get it cleaned? Her underwear she stuffed in the back pack, along with her bra. Those were also apparently useless here. She wondered what women did when they got their periods here. What did they wear? Human women used to use old rags, leaves or bark.

She moved the torch back into the hallway. It was too hot to look at it closely. What made it burn for such a long time?

Then she went back into the cave and crawled beneath a delicious layer of the soft furs. Her mind went over and over the day's events.

Wouldn't her boss be surprised when she didn't show up for work tomorrow? That would seal everything. She'd lose her job without a fight.

What if she never got back home?

She wasn't missing much. Her life there had been

meaningless. She wouldn't be missed. She'd spoken more today than she had in the entire last year.

It seemed to take hours to go to sleep. She worried about the coming move Mala had talked about. Would she be invited to come along?

Normally, she wanted people to leave her alone. But not here. Not in this strange place.

She didn't know how to find food. And what about the hurracha she'd met in that meadow? She didn't want to meet it again. This was a dangerous world.

She wouldn't live long alone.

And Penelope found, for the first time in her life, that she wanted to live.

CHAPTER 2 - TAVOR

TAVOR LEANED ON THE SMOOTH HANDLED HOE, LOOKING AT HIS handiwork. He knew he wasn't weeding fast enough. His mother wouldn't be pleased. But then again, she never was. Not with him.

She was ashamed of him. Ashamed of herself for going with a man who was one of the Moon People. A raider. Even though the man had brought her deer meat now and again. And even once a bear carcass.

His mother hated him, but soon he would be gone. His twelfth summer was coming and the Moon People would be passing by again. He was old enough to be allowed to go to them now. Then he'd be beyond the taunts of the other kids.

He'd become a raider, just like his father. And he'd come back here and steal everything worth while. Every precious valuable they had. He'd even steal his mother's sewing needles. He'd steal her new partner's, Joam's, fattest pig. He'd steal the metal worker's finest blade.

He'd show them all that he was worth something.

No matter what they thought.

He hated the Day People, even though he was a mix. He should never have been born.

What had his father been thinking?

Tavor would never father a child. Never. He wanted nothing more to do with one drop of Day People's blood and any child he had would still be part Day People.

Day People were pigs who groveled in the dirt, trying to scratch out grubs. They never moved, always staying in the same place. Using up the same land, fouling the same water again and again.

The Moon People were cleaner. Spending winter in one place, summer in another. They hunted and fished for food. Occasionally they traded with the Day People for what they needed. More often, they just took it and left fresh meat or fish.

The Day People couldn't hunt even if it meant saving their own lives. Fresh game was only out at night and the Day People were afraid to go out at night. When the sun disappeared from the sky, they locked themselves inside their homes.

The Moon People followed the moons, the pale blue of Eesia and Ananna. Twin sisters who crossed the sky in search of their families. At least that's what the Day People thought. What the Moon People thought must be absolutely different. They were better, stronger and could see in the dark, just like him.

"Tavor, have you finished the weeding yet?" came his mother's voice from around the corner of the house. She must be hanging up the clean laundry.

"Not yet," he said, getting back to hoeing the weeds out of the vegetables.

"Well, you'd better hurry. There's a lot of work that needs to be done before sunset and I can't do it all."

He snorted. And continued working. Their garden bordered the lane. If he looked down it, he knew he'd see several boys his age goofing off and wrestling in the common pasture. They were allowed to tend their families' cows and goats. His mother didn't have any. Why had she got herself hooked up with a man who raised pigs? Probably because he was the only one who'd live with her after she mated with a Moon Person. And got a child their enemy.

Even his mother would be better off once Tavor was gone. And he didn't want her to be better off.

He hated her.

He hated them all.

And he wasn't sure that he'd like the Moon People any better. They probably hated mixes just as much as the day people.

He'd find out soon enough.

CHAPTER 3 - PENELOPE

Groggily, Penelope rolled over. Her pillow felt extra soft this morning. So did her bed. So cozy and it was still dark, except for a lamp on the far side of the room.

Why was someone trying to wake her up?

She lived alone.

Who would be around to wake her up?

"Hypatia, wake up," said Mala. "It's time to eat, aren't you hungry."

Penelope rolled over and looked at the woman. It took several moments before she could figure out who Mala was and where they were.

So, it wasn't a dream. Somehow this really was happening. She'd ended up in a different world. And told them her name was Hypatia.

Why had she done that?

And here she was sleeping in furs, stark naked. She'd never slept naked a night in her life.

Penelope scrambled out of the soft furs and grabbed the

tunic, slipping it on. Then she pulled on the leather boots and tied them.

"You should leave them off, let your feet grow hard."

"I know. But I don't think I can face hard rocks before breakfast."

Mala laughed.

Penelope followed her through the tunnels trying to memorize the route Mala took, but soon, she was hopelessly lost again. The inside of this mountain was a maze of caves and corridors. Even though the tunnels felt different. Some were damper than others, some cooler. Others smelled like food or like moist earth.

Finally, they were in the large cavern with the tables. A lot of people were already eating. Penelope counted at least a hundred. She grabbed a wooden bowl and stood behind Mala.

"There's cooked oats, we got them from the village the other night. Oh look, someone has been harvesting the first of the spring berries. And make sure you get some nuts on it."

Mala sprinkled a handful of berries and nuts over her oats, then splashed some milk from a jug over the whole thing. She picked up a spoon and headed for a table.

Penelope copied her and sat down next to her.

She took a spoonful of the oats and berries. The oats tasted like uncooked oatmeal and the berries were tart and almost spicy. The milk tasted very peculiar. It wasn't from a cow, she knew that much. But all in all, it was a fairly good meal.

A man came by with a metal pot and poured greenish liquid into their wooden cups. Penelope hadn't seen much metal since she arrived here. The metal pot must have been taken from the village.

"What is this?" Penelope asked Mala.

"Probably striped grass tea. We collect the grass in the summer, dry it and then make tea from it."

Penelope sipped it. It tasted like bland herb tea. Not very interesting. But then she never drank tea or coffee with breakfast. Her parents never let her and when she moved out on her own, she just never picked up the habit.

"What are we doing today?" asked Penelope, finally getting up the nerve.

She was used to having control of her time. Planning out what books needed minor repairs, which ones needed complete rebinding in order to save them. Used to working alone.

Mala looked at her and said, "Today we leave for our summer camp."

"Don't you need to pack?" asked Penelope.

"Pack? We just pick things up and go. Whatever we can't carry is left behind. We will be back before winter."

"What about people who can't walk?"

"We have no such people right now. But when we do, we make a chair for them and they are carried. The people who carry them, their loads are distributed to others willing to help. Those with children too young to walk, their loads are carried with others, so they many carry their children." She paused, cocking her head. "Every now and then we have someone who is dying, too ill to come along, or they wish to die where they are. Then a few people stay with them and come later, when they can."

Penelope nodded.

"What should I bring?"

"Your cup, spoon and bowl, clothes and a few sleeping furs. It's warmer where we stay in summer than it is in the caves."

The caves felt hot to her already. How hot would their summer camp get? They must live in the tropics here.

She couldn't figure out if it was a different planet or a different world. She obviously wasn't on Earth anymore, even though certain things were familiar. People drank out of cups and slept on furs, there were chickens and oats.

Mala had finished eating and she said, "Come, I'll help you decide what to take."

Penelope followed her back to her room in a cave that smelled like the sweet rushes, and they went through the clothes. In the end she took only three tunics. She sadly set aside her T-shirt, jeans, underwear and running shoes. Not because she wouldn't need them. But they were part of her old life, which a small part of her wanted to go back to, but mostly she wanted to leave behind.

That life was relatively safe. Not much unexpected happened. She generally knew what her days would be like. Except for the recent threat of losing her job, she'd been doing the same thing in the same way for over thirty years.

She was competent at it and actually, book repair hadn't changed that much in a very long time. Except there were fewer positions available as the libraries turned more and more to digital books and computers.

Here, she had a chance to become a new person. A chance to survive and prove to herself that she wasn't just wasted space. Which she'd so often felt like back in her old life.

She decided to leave her backpack behind as well. She didn't want to stand out among these people any more than she already did. She rolled up the belongings she was taking in the largest sleeping fur with a soft rope. Making straps like Mala shower her, to carry it on her back. And the book she'd been reading, well, it was pretty unforgettable. She put it in her backpack. She'd look at it again when they returned, in winter.

They took the rest of the furs and clothes and draped them over a rope, which was tied through holes someone had chiseled out of the rock long ago and strung across the cave. To keep things dry and mostly bug free, Mala told her.

Penelope clipped her backpack to the rope and tied her running shoes together and strung them up as well.

Then they removed all the rushes and dumped them on a pile outside the mountain. Penelope was surprised to see that it was dusk. Inside the mountain everything was light enough. She'd just gotten up, so expected it to be daytime outside.

Everyone else was bringing their rushes as well.

"We give everything back to the land," she said. "Birds will come and carry them away for nests, other creatures will come and take them. The summer winds will blow them away and they will enrich the soil where they settle."

Penelope followed Mala to her own quarters, which consisted of one large cave with several shelves. It had a sweet smell of warm bodies and felt homey.

Mala's partner, Amuna rolled up furs and clothes in bundles to take along. The floor was already cleared of rushes.

Penelope hadn't expected to see two women as partners. But why should this world be that different than her own? Perhaps people were people everywhere.

Penelope helped hang up the things being left behind.

Dall, Mala's son couldn't do much with one arm. His other arm was tied to his body, immobilized like a sling. Penelope guessed he was almost a teenager, but wasn't sure. She'd never been around young kids much as an adult.

"How is he?" asked Penelope.

"His fever is gone. That is good. It will take time before his arm is healed and he can use it again."

"I'm happy for him."

Amuna had finished making bundles to carry. She slung a bow and quiver of arrows over her muscular shoulder, then tied what looked like a long knife in a sheath around her waist. She looked formiddable

"I must go. We will meet you at the first stopping place."

They kissed and Amuna moved towards the door.

"May you always find abundant game," said Mala.

"May your burdens be always light," Amuna replied and was gone.

Mala said, "The hunters travel on ahead of us, so we don't scare away their prey." She smiled, her large teeth shining in the light of the glowing rocks. "That way we get to eat."

They helped Dall get a small bundle on his back and Mala took two bundles, hers and Amuna's.

"Do you need help?" asked Penelope.

"No, they are not heavy. We Moon People have learned to travel light."

Then they went out of the cave.

Into the complete darkness.

It took a while for Penelope's eyes to adjust. It wasn't absolutely dark. There were stars and the light of two moons. She could make out shapes and the path. One of the moons was full, the other about two thirds full. Or maybe it wasn't a fully round moon. Was that possible?

Most of the time she could see. Sometimes the tall trees shaded the path.

She followed Mala and Dall into the forest, relieved and thankful she had boots on. Still the swipes of ferns and bushes on her mostly bare legs and arms made her shiver. She tried not to think about what sort of bugs might be on them.

Everyone walked single file and she had to work hard to keep up with the group.

Strange cries came from the trees above, but whether they were from birds or something else, she didn't know. The sounds followed the path, keeping pace with the large group of people, as if warning of the intruders' presence.

The air smelled fresh and felt cool, as if after a rain, although the brush they moved through didn't feel wet.

Penelope had no idea what this world was like. Or this part of the world. She'd spent her few days and nights here inside a mountain.

She felt it when they moved out into a meadow. Everything opened up and became lighter. She could even see her shadow from the moons. They rose high in the sky, the smaller blue one following the larger yellowish moon, the one that was full.

The meadow stretched on for what looked like miles. But then it wouldn't be a meadow, would it? That would make it a plain or something. Penelope didn't know the difference. She wasn't an outdoorsy type.

Penelope could see the huge mass of people traveling. Now that they were out of the forest most were about five abreast. She stopped counting at 185. There were at least that many people behind her. The knee high grasses were flattened by the time she got there. How many people had lived in that mountain?

Occasionally, someone wearing a bow and a quiver of arrows or a long spear, as well as a sheathed knife would race up and down the side of the column. Looking outwards. For what? Or whom? Who would dare to attack a mass of people this large?

Then she remembered watching a documentary on the migration of caribou across the tundra. Packs of wolves would wait for a straggler, a sick older caribou or a young one who wandered too far from the herd. And they'd be on it, dragging it farther away from the herd and it'd be dead.

What were the guards looking for?

She'd ask Mala when she caught up with her.

The younger woman walked a couple of rows ahead of her, trying to keep up with her son, who asked continual questions. Since no one else was speaking, Penelope could hear them all, even though he was asking quietly.

"When will we be there?"

"When we get there," Mala patiently replied.

"How long will that be?"

"Six to seven nights."

"Why do we have to go so far to the summer camp?"

"Because that's the safest place that's close enough that has enough game to feed all of us."

"What will we eat?"

"Antelope, deer, many, many kinds of fish and there will be many berries."

"Berries, I love berries."

There was silence for a time.

"Will the Day People near there be nicer to us?"

"Day People go about their lives as they will. They're awake during the day when we sleep and they sleep at night when we're awake. There is room for all of us in this world. But I don't think you'll see many of them. They don't live near our summer camp."

"Why?"

"Why what?"

"Why do they sleep at night? The world is so beautiful then."

"Yes it is, but their eyes are different. They can't see at night like we can. They see only the stars and the moons, not the plants and the animals. They work all day; growing food, taking care of their animals and making things and they sleep inside at night."

"What do they make?"

"They make metals and swords. They make material for the clothes you're wearing."

"Not my boots." He stomped proudly.

"No, not your boots, but I think they do make boots."

"Why don't they travel like we do?"

"They don't hunt, they keep animals. And they feed the soil so their plants will always grow. They don't need to hunt or forage for food. We are so many that after a season we need to move, so the plants can recover and the animals will return. Then when we come back, there will be food again."

"I don't like fish."

She laughed. "I didn't either when I was your age. But I like it now."

Noise and excitement erupted from the front of the line. Penelope couldn't see that far. Everyone stopped. Most of the warriors ran to the front. It surprised her that some of the warriors were women. They looked as fierce and strong as the men. Some of them carried spears as well as bow and arrow.

It turned out they were passing a village of the Day People. They had a guard out and people had rushed out of their homes to defend the village. Their town brought the stink of manure to her nose.

Mala said, "We've only taken when in need. The Day People don't know how to trade. Usually, we bring meat we've hunted or plants from the deep forest in exchange for what we take from them. It is a fair trade."

How did the Day People view the situation? Apparently much differently.

The entire line passed by their village and the Moon People's warriors stood facing the armed Day People the entire time.

The Day People wore fabric clothing. Baggy shirts and pants with leather boots. They had belts around their tunics with silver swords or knives, sheathed on them. At least some were sheathed. Their eyes were smaller than the Moon People. More human looking. They looked a little browner than the pale Moon People. Obviously they spent more time in the sunlight. Their hair was cut short.

The women were clustered behind the wooden buildings, not close to the trail. They were too far away for her to see them well. The wore tunics over long skirts, had their long hair tied back or put up on their heads. All she could see were their outlines.

Penelope stopped and stared at the silent confrontation. She shivered at the hatred in the Day People's eyes. She could see their anger in the moonlight. The kind of misunderstanding or belittlement she'd seen all her life. She had always been the other. The one who never fit it. The one people made fun of behind her back.

It made her feel small.

She shrank back into the line and began walking again. Trying to be invisible. It felt safer that way.

"You are new here, I believe," said a young man, carrying a toddler on his shoulders.

"Yes," she said.

"It has always been this way. They do not understand us. My father's father told me that for a very long time, we tried to make them understand. Then we gave up."

"But is giving up any better? Where will that lead?"

"I don't know. I didn't like that the Elders gave up. But I have not been fighting that battle for as long as they have. It must be disappointing."

She nodded.

Penelope trudged on through the night. They stopped a couple of times for food and water, but mostly they walked endlessly. By the time dawn came along, she felt exhausted and her legs ached all the way down to her bones.

When they stopped, she unfolded her sleeping furs and collapsed inside them. She slept restlessly; her legs cramped throughout the day until someone woke her.

Dusk was coming. People stirred from their sleep and

began eating. Breakfast, or was it dinner, consisted of more dried meat and water. The same as they'd eaten all night while walking. She was thinking that's what the menu would consist of until they got to the summer camp.

The group moved slowly for about half the night. One of the women was in labor. They walked as long as she wanted to. Stopping when she stopped.

When they stopped for good, the line shifted into a circular mass. Penelope unrolled her furs and sat on them. She wasn't sleepy, just tired. Her legs ached from a night and a half of walking. She rubbed her calves and watched the people around her.

Penelope sat near the center of the circle, and a group of five old women. She'd been following them for several hours and noticed the warriors often came and asked them questions or gave them information.

They sat cross legged, in a circle, silent with their eyes closed. In the dark they seemed continually caught in beams of moonlight.

But there was something else.

It was as if light emanated from them. And gradually, the illumination widened, encompassing the whole group of people.

Before the light began spreading there had been a lot of chatter. As the glow widened, silence drifted over the crowd, as if the light spread a feeling of calm and peace. The only sound to be heard was the moaning of the woman in labor and the whispering of the people encouraging her.

Penelope had never had children, never felt 'adult' enough to have one. Even if she'd had a partner, which she never had. Here she was, nearly sixty and still a virgin. Never wanted to be with a man. Never wanted to be with anyone.

People weren't to be trusted.

Yet here in this strange world, completely dependent upon others.

The irony of it made her smile.

Finally, there was a sobbing of joy, people near the woman in labor began cooing at the new baby.

Penelope felt a wave of relief flow over the crowd. Her mouth dropped open. Never had she been in a group of people and felt the same thing as others.

She looked around to see people smiling.

The old women broke their silence and began whispering to each other.

"What did you see?" asked a woman wearing an orange headscarf.

"I saw problems at the gap, Sian," said a woman wearing a calf-length royal blue tunic.

"Bears?" asked another, her long hair in intricate braids. Penelope remembered her being called Solia.

"Day People," said the woman in blue. Her name was Casia

"So, it has come," said the last one, the one who looked older than the others. Tassora, that was her name.

"Yes, I believe it has," said the woman in blue.

"We are not ready," said the woman in the scarf.

"We never are," said the eldest.

"How should we prepare?" asked the one with braids.

"We should take another road," said the woman in blue.

"Is that what you saw?" asked the eldest.

The woman in the blue tunic shook her head.

"Then that is not the solution," said the eldest. "The road would simply shift and put us back at the pass. No. We must meet it head on. We must confront the Day People."

"Fight them?" asked the one with braids.

"No. That is not the way. We must confront them. The five

of us. They are not cowardly. They will not hurt unarmed Elders."

Penelope felt relieved that the women weren't planning on a battle.

What exactly had she walked into when she got off that bus?

She didn't think that five old women were going to talk sense into the Day People though.

They wouldn't have had much effect on the group they passed so far. They'd been ready to attack the Moon People. And she wasn't sure the next village would be any different.

Penelope didn't really understand this place at all.

She wished she were back home. Even with a job that might vanish. Or perhaps enough time had passed in her world that her job had already vanished because she hadn't shown up for work. How did this going to another world thing work anyway?

Was this like in all those fantasies she'd read where the character went into another world and once they'd learned what they had to then they got to go back home? A doorway simply opened?

What was it that she was supposed to learn here?

To get along with other people? To not be afraid? No chance of those happening. To stand up for herself? The thought of doing that made her shrink farther into herself. She had no idea what she was supposed to learn. Which was why she probably wouldn't learn anything.

And she'd never get home.

After the meal, she lay on her furs, pulling more of them over the top of her. She'd never slept outside. Never gone camping. Not even as a kid. She'd convinced herself that she wouldn't be able to sleep out in nature. But she was exhausted from all the exercise and slept soundly, missing the sunrise.

Penelope woke in the afternoon, felt the heat from the sun blazing down.

Everyone else lay sleeping, except for a few warriors. She went back to sleep until others stirred, eating breakfast. Dusk fell and the darkness enveloped them like fog.

That night she felt the land they walked on change. The grassy plains fell away and they began to climb. She felt sorry for the new mother, who probably wasn't up for climbing, but the young woman looked happy, carrying her baby in a fur wrapped around her still heavy body. The baby mostly slept.

As they walked Penelope felt the air grow cooler and the ground beneath her feet became solid rock. The smells of prairie weeds and grasses diminished, replaced by the pungent scent of short conifers. She didn't know what the trees were, but they were only about ten feet tall and slightly gnarled.

The group was moving up into the feet of mountains.

They climbed for two more days before the foothills leveled out. Penelope had never walked so much in her entire life. Her feet felt gnarled and crampy like old tree roots. She'd just begun to get used to walking when the climbing began. Now she ached all over again.

The older women began collecting plants: tubers of a plant they called all-heal, the roots of a certain grass to make dye and the new leaves of yet another plant they used for tea.

Every morning she fell into her furs, exhausted from the night's walking.

When she'd wake, Penelope noticed that not everyone slept the whole day through. The old women got up about halfway through the day and began working on various things. Laying out the leaves and roots to dry or dying wool taken from the day people. They were a hub of industry.

The next day Penelope couldn't sleep. She woke after only a

few hours and lay tossing. It was going to be a hot day and she felt smothered beneath the furs.

Without the furs, flies annoyed her, landing on her just as she drifted off. They were huge and they bit, leaving nasty red welts. And they were everywhere.

Finally, she got up and walked around. One of the old woman, nodded at her and went back to cooking roots in water, making some sort of dye.

Penelope left the encampment and walked into a nearby grove of trees, appreciating the coolness. The chatter of birds filled the air, cackles and coos, screeches and soft chirrups. The foliage of trees and bushes looked luminous in the sun and everything smelled like wet soil. She inhaled, feeling thankful for the freshness.

The birds broke out into a cacophony. There was a swarm of small birds, chasing a larger one. A big black bird, too large to be a crow. All of a sudden it swooped down towards her and landed on her right shoulder, folding its wings in and preening.

"Not a crow, I'm a raven." She heard his harsh voice in her mind. She wasn't sure why she felt it was a he, it just seemed right.

"Did you just speak to me."

He looked at her right eye and cocked its head, studying her.

"Ow, please don't claw me. This fabric is very thin," she said.

"Sorry. It wasn't my intention to hurt you." Again, he spoke silently, in her mind.

She shook her head, trying to clear it.

Penelope asked, "Were you the same bird who warned me to run, the first day I came here?"

"Yes," he said.

"Why? Why did you help me?" she asked.

"You were so pathetic, I took pity on you."

"Why me?"

"You have work to do," he said.

"Me? What sort of work do I have to do?"

"It's been a very long time since this group of people have had a wisdom keeper. I think you'd do well."

"What's a wisdom keeper?"

"Someone who remembers all the stories and all the wisdom that everyone's discovered. Someone who will write it down and teach others. The Moon People will need that to avoid a war."

"I don't have that good of a memory," she said. Penelope didn't want a job. She just wanted to go on as she had. "And I can't prevent a war."

She felt horrified at the thought of such violence.

Now would be a good time to go home.

"You can write. You come from another world where people write. You need to write things down. And teach others to write and read."

"I'm not a teacher," she said.

"Well, you'd better become one. And fast This is very important. I wouldn't demand it otherwise." He squawked at her.

"I don't know how to begin," Penelope said. Her gut was all rolled up like a ball of nerves. She didn't need any more challenges. It was hard enough to be in a strange worlds and around so many people.

"Walk back to the encampment."

"Okay," she said. She grudgingly turned around and left the grove of trees. It didn't take long to walk back, but every step was painful. The raven's claws dug into her shoulder. She could see a bit of blood dripping down it.

How was it she was talking to a bird? And doing what he said?

This couldn't really be happening.

But the claws in her shoulder ripped her out of her thoughts and back into her body. She could deny it till the sky turned green, but this was happening.

She was in a different world after all.

The old woman wearing the orange headscarf, who'd been making dyes, looked up at her in surprise.

The raven dug in one last time, causing Penelope to cry out from the searing pain.

It flew away calling back to her, "I'll return tomorrow."

She crumpled to the ground near the old woman.

"Oh dear, dear. We'll have to do something about those wounds. You sit still. I've got some salve that will help," the woman said.

She scurried over to a woven bag and rummaged around in it until she found the right container. Pulling out a small clay bottle, she removed the top, a string wrapped around a large, shiny leaf. Then dipped her fingers in it.

"This will help clean the wounds and help them heal," she said, smearing the salve onto Penelope's skin. The salve smelled so pungent it cleared Penelope's nose.

The old woman said, "We can't have you getting sick. So, you've been chosen by a raven? That's very impressive. What does it want you to do?"

"It said something about wanting me to be a wisdom keeper, but I don't know how I can do that," Penelope said. "I have no wisdom, whatsoever."

"That will come or perhaps you have more wisdom than you realize. There, let the salve soak in for a little while. I believe I have just the piece of fur you'll need to protect your shoulder."

The salve cooled her torn skin.

Penelope watched as the woman dug through a different bag. She pulled out a small piece of brown fur and a woven cord.

The woman tied a piece of clean cotton cloth onto her shoulder to cover the wound and then the fur over it. It felt comforting.

"What's your name?" asked Penelope.

"I am Sian."

"I'm Penelope."

"Mala told us your name was Hypatia."

"That's what I told her. It's really Penelope," she said, looking down.

"You are going through a transformation, one of many I believe. I think you should choose a name that feels right and use that one."

Penelope was her birth name. She'd always hated it. It's meaning said 'a web over her face'. It had suited her old life, helped her hide. Hypatia had been a mathematician, an astronomer and a philosopher. And a teacher.

"Call me Hypatia."

"Ah, I thought so. How did the raven tell you to keep our people's wisdom?"

"He wants me to write it down."

"You know how to write?" the old woman asked, staring at her, mouth hanging open and eyes wide.

"Yes, I do. Where I come from, everyone knows how to read and write."

"It must be an amazing place," the old woman said, stirring her clay pot of dye. Using the stirring stick, she raised the fabric being dyed, checked the color and returned it to the pot.

"But what will I write on?"

"We make paper from reeds grown at our summer camp. I

do believe Casia might still have some with her. She paints on it."

"And what about ink? What do I write with?" asked Hypatia. She had a feeling there was no getting out of this.

"Well, we have paint. And dyes. You could probably use a sharp stick. One that will absorb some of the color."

Hypatia crumpled over slightly.

"Sometimes we are called on to do things we're not ready for. We need to grow into the role. You will do fine."

"I hope so," said Hypatia. "Thank you for your help."

"You are most welcome. I'm glad I could help. You should go rest now. We have a long march ahead of us when the moons rise. I'll put more salve on when you wake up. And give you a piece of fur to tie over your shoulder.

Hypatia went to her furs and lay down. Her shoulder throbbed, but not as much as before the salve. She replayed the discussion with the raven over and over again. Before she fell asleep a plan began forming in her mind.

CHAPTER 4 - TAVOR

THE MEN IN THE VILLAGE WERE CLUSTERED INSIDE THE MEETING building. Tavor sat on the ground outside the open window. The one on the far side, where he wouldn't be noticed. He chewed a piece of wheat stalk and leaned against the rough wood, his hat pushed down just below his eyebrows, pretending to be asleep. Drops of sweat rolled down his temples from the heat of the day, but he didn't brush them away.

Tavor also ignored the blood flies, good thing he wore long sleeves and pants. They were worse than normal this year. But they only came out during the day. They must not bother the Moon People.

Behind the meeting building stood an empty field of weeds. It used to be someone's garden, but had been abandoned for at least two years by the look of it.

No one came back this way.

He listened intently to the battle raging inside.

"I think you are wrong," said Mase. His voice deeper than

the others. "As long as we let them, they will trespass on our lands."

"And how are these our lands?" said a voice Tavor recognized as Elias. The man spent his life thinking and teaching. "Who granted us the complete right to everything that lives in this world?"

"Our hard work," said someone. "We work the soil, plant the seeds and make things grow."

"We do not make things grow. The sun and the rain do that. The seeds themselves contain their own destiny," said Elias again.

"We tend this land and our animals. We make the metal into knives and tools. Our women weave the fabric. The Moon People steal everything." Mace again, his voice growing louder.

"They also leave behind meat. And healing herbs. And delicacies from the forest, mushrooms, berries and such. Have you asked them if they consider what they're doing stealing? I believe they would see it as trading," said Elias.

Elias' voice remained calm. He clearly wasn't trying to start a fight, unlike Mace.

Tavor loved to listen to or watch a good fight. But he didn't want to see any harm come to the Moon People.

"We don't need their leavings," said another.

"Oh, but you do, Amuler. It was their herbs that saved your son when he was sick last winter from the choking death. And your wife Mase, when she nearly bled to death after the birth of your daughter. Do none of you remember any of this?" asked Elias.

"But we could get the herbs ourselves. They don't pay for what is stolen."

"But we can't get them ourselves. The healers have said they don't know how to find the herbs or where they grow. And it was only because the Moon People showed us how to use the herbs to save people we hadn't known how to help before," said Elias.

There was murmuring amongst the men. Elias was gaining ground on Mase.

"They still take too much. And they take our women. Get them with child and leave us with half bloods," said a voice he recognized as the man his mother had married.

Mase jumped in. "And none of us would want to touch their disgusting women, so it's just too much. I say we teach them that this bear bites. We've been patient long enough letting them steal what we need for survival. They've been spotted already. Let's kill a few of them. Up at the pass. We'll form an ambush."

"And then what will happen?" asked Elias. "Do you think they'll bow down and say, "Oh we'll never take what we need again? Is that what you would do Mase?"

"Uh, yes," said Mase, but the uncertainty was in his voice.

Tavor heard footsteps coming towards him, but didn't move. The hot sun streamed down on him, baking his feet in his boots and his head beneath the straw hat.

He felt a shadow fall on him, and the stink of another person's sweat, but remained still except for breathing deeply. In, out, in, out. Pretending he was asleep.

The person snorted and walked off, as if in disgust.

Tavor cracked his eyes to see Jase, Mase's son. One of his enemies. Why hadn't Jase taken the opportunity to harass him? Call him to the attention of the men inside?

But Jase kept walking.

That meant he was planning something worse.

He'd missed a bit of the conversation. Especially Elias' response. Plans were being made. The ambushers would be leaving in the morning.

Tavor rose slowly as if waking from a nap. He went around

the other side of the building, the opposite direction that Jase went. He didn't want a fight. Not right now.

He wanted to go home and pull his few pathetic belongings together. And get some food. Then head off into the surrounding forest. He could travel all night. The ambushers couldn't do that. Not easily at least.

He'd warn the Moon People and join them. It was time to take his place in their world. And get out of this miserable village.

But first he'd create a few diversions.

Tonight.

CHAPTER 5 - HYPATIA

Hypatia walked along the matted grass trail, Raven on her shoulder. On the fur piece protecting her shoulder. Between using the salve and the fur, her shoulder didn't hurt anymore.

It was dark, with the moons chasing each other over the sky above. Stars of all sizes glittered in between. A cool breeze blew across the plains and up towards the mountains, removing the overwhelming heat of the day and making her feel more comfortable. The air brought with it the scent of the particularly pungent bushes that grew nearby.

Raven spoke continually in her mind. His raucous voice in constant conversation with her. Mostly, she listened, occasionally, she questioned.

"Why do I need to memorize the stories, if I'm writing them down?"

"It's part of their world. They won't listen to you until you can prove your worth somehow. It's part of gaining their trust, their confidence."

The group of five women, one of whom was Sian, another

Casia, walked in front of her. They were still debating the best method of dealing with the Day People.

The thought of any kind of confrontation made Hypatia want to curl up into a ball and hide.

"You should not be afraid of confrontation."

"But I am?"

"Why?"

"I don't want to get hurt or die."

"That is part of life. We get hurt every day. If you were not alive, you could not die. You've spent far too much of your time being barely alive, hiding in the shadows. You must come fully alive."

"Just how do I do that?" she asked, annoyed.

"Release your fears. One by one. Name your fear. Envision it surrounded by a cloud and watch it drift away in the sky. When they are gone, you will find the clarity about how to live. Your fears smother you."

She practiced releasing her fears through the rest of the night's walk.

Hypatia envisioned herself at work, listening to her coworker in the break room, chatting and laughing together. She let go of her fear of talking to others.

Farther down the trail, she let go of the fear of eating alone in a restaurant. She pictured herself going into the Indian restaurant which always smelled so good when she passed it. She went in, sat down at a table and ordered. Then enjoyed the most wonderful food, which tasted much better than any curry she bought at the grocery store.

How could there be so many fears? And some were so large they just kept reappearing.

They camped in a lightly forested area on a rise. She could see the land below turn a lavender shade as the sun began to rise. Placing her fur beneath a tree, Hypatia dropped onto it like a backpack full of too many books. Her legs were tired.

She was nearly asleep when one of the servers for the night brought her a bowl of roasted meat which made her mouth water from just smelling it. She didn't ask what kind. The hunters had been lucky.

She put a small pile of the meat on the ground and Raven ate it quickly, asking for more.

"If I give you too much you won't be able to fly."

"Why do I need to fly? I have you to carry me."

"You'll need to move quickly if arrows start flying up at the pass."

"That's two nights away," he said.

She slowly chewed the juicy meat. It was cooked perfectly. These days she felt so hungry from all the walking. Her muscles had gotten much stronger. She'd probably only been five or ten pounds overweight. Just pudgy and soft. That had certainly changed. Her body felt strong and more capable than it had since before she was a teenager. But she hadn't been paying attention then.

Now she was.

Although she still felt tired. Listening and talking to Raven all day wore her out.

"I'm going to sleep now," she said.

"Good. I need to be alone," he squawked.

She watched as the bird finished her meat and flew up into the trees above.

Hypatia curled up in her furs and was soon lost in sleep.

She woke early again and spent time with the old women. They were the ones who told her stories.

But today they had something else in mind.

"We're going to teach you how to hold power," said Sian.

"Hold power?" she asked, chewing on cold meat from the previous meal.

"Yes. We'll need your help at the pass," said Tassora. She was the eldest of the women. And the strongest. It was as if every day she lived, her body and mind grew more robust and powerful.

Completely contrary to the world Hypatia came from.

Hypatia still felt afraid of the coming confrontation, but she couldn't see herself ever arguing with Tassora. No one did, she'd noticed. Not one person. Not once Tassora had stated a position.

"What do I do?" Hypatia asked.

"This is very simple," said Casia. She was the one who had dreams and vision. Easy for her to say it was simple. "Sit facing inwards for right now."

Hypatia faced them and crossed her legs, since that's what they were doing. Then they all joined hands.

"Close your eyes," said Tassora. "And clear your mind of everything except what I am saying. Feel your rear against the soft soil of this land. Feel the season after season of leaves and needles which have fallen to the ground and broken into many pieces. Making food for the trees. Feel your roots growing into this soft soil as if you were a part of this grove. Choose whatever type of tree feels right for you. Your roots grow deeper and deeper, seeking the water which runs deep in the rock of these mountains. Your roots anchor you here until you are as solid as the mountain. Then from your roots grows a seedling, bursting forth from beneath the soil into the moonlight and sunlight. You grow upwards, adding branch after branch, needle or leaf after needle or leaf. Growing taller, while your roots grow deeper and wider, entwining with those of the trees surrounding you. Feel the vibrancy of your body. Every leaf or needle touched by a breeze. Your bark basking in the light of the moons and the sun. Your roots sharing energy with the other trees and the water and soil surrounding this forest. Feel that energy rise up through your roots and your trunk, traveling into your branches. Feel it mingle with the light of the moon, the touch of the wind, the patter of rain. Feel all that energy connect and balance. And hold that feeling. There will be subtle shifts, but hold that energy. Keep it strong and flowing. Feel it spread to the surrounding trees, feel it mingle with theirs until this circle of trees is joined in that energy. It flows everywhere around us."

Then Tassora fell silent.

Hypatia felt the peace and vibrancy of being a tree. Felt the energy swirling around her and let it happen. She felt a surge of energy from Tassora, but focused on keeping the energy flowing.

Finally, Tassora said, "Now take your energy and move back into your tree. Feel the sap running, the moonlight on your leaves or needles. Put your hands on the ground and feel the rich soil at your feet. Let all that energy flow back into the mountain beneath you."

Hypatia put her hands on the dirt and felt the energy dissipate. Enough of the energy stayed with her, causing her to feel more alive than she ever had.

"Open your eyes," said Tassora.

Hypatia opened her eyes.

The entire group of moon people stood or sat upright in a circle around them. Completely silent. She hadn't heard any of them move.

"Well, I think that went really well," said Tassora. "I believe if we practice this for the next two nights, we'll be ready for the Day People. Hypatia you make a strong addition to our circle."

"Thank you," she said. No one had ever told her she was strong.

Hypatia looked around at the other women. Each of them looked like she felt. Alive and filled with energy.

Then she looked at the crowd who had gathered around them. They looked the same.

"Our people have been wakened by the energy we rose. I poured some of it into them. Some hope and strength. They will need it as we get closer to the pass," Tassora said. "And it was good to be able to do that. At the pass, again I will leave the circle to use that energy. But against our enemies."

"How?" asked Hypatia.

"I don't know. I will have to see what presents itself," said Tassora.

CHAPTER 6 - TAVOR

Tavor silently slid into Mase's storage outbuilding. It smelled musty. High up on a wooden shelf to the right sat metal jugs of cooking oil. He grabbed four of them, then slid back out the door. He stooped under the weight and walked quietly. Everyone was asleep.

He went to every building in the village, except one, and poured oil around the base of them, wetting the wood with the thick oil. This batch of oil was made from hassa nuts. He could smell the deep, rich scent.

He left Elias' home safe.

They wouldn't accuse Elias of doing such a thing. Once Tavor was found missing, they'd figure it out.

Everyone hated him as much as he did them.

He was a half blood, one of the Moon People. One of *them*.

Once all the buildings were wet with oil, he took an unlit torch into his house and put it into the hearth, where it caught fire.

Then he went outside and started lighting the oil. Smoke

blossomed everywhere, catching in his throat. Making it hard to see.

The last house done, he dropped the torch and walked to the grove of trees on the far side of town, listening as the screams began and people began running out of their houses. He could see the terror on their faces.

He could hear the crackling of dried wood burning. Flames swallowed buildings before they could be put out. A beam cracked in his mother's house and the whole thing caved in. The town was filled with light even though the moons weren't out yet. People were running, yelling, trying to get each other out of buildings. Bringing buckets of water to others.

None of them would have helped him. No one would have tried to rescue him. He didn't count.

Smoke plumed up from the town and the wind blew it in his direction. He choked on the smell of roasted meat and wood smoke.

Tavor pulled his pack from the tree where he'd stashed it and walked away.

Done.

He had taken his revenge and felt cleansed.

CHAPTER 7 - HYPATIA

IT WAS TOWARDS DAWN OF THE NEXT DAY WHEN THEY STOPPED
to rest. The sky was lightening into a blush pink moving
towards blue. Hypatia's mouth felt full of dust and sand gritted
between her teeth.

One of the hunters brought forward a boy he'd come upon.
The boy demanded to be presented to the man in charge.

Apparently, the hunter had laughed at him.

The boy, enraged, attacked him and was quickly taken
down and tied up.

Now the hunter, Amuna, Mala's partner, stood before the
six elders, asking what should be done. The boy stood in front
of him, hands tied behind his back. He looked like the Moon
People. But said he was from a village of Day People.

Hypatia was puzzled by this until Casia explained that
children who had a parent from each group lived with the
mother until coming of age. Then they could choose where
to go.

Sian asked, "What is your name, boy?"

"Tavor. Why am I talking to you old women?"

"Because we are 'in charge,'" said Sian, raising her eyebrows.

"But you're old women," he said, sputtering. "You can't be in charge."

"We are not foolish Day People," said Casia, "who only see the worth of half our number."

That shut him up. Hypatia could almost see him thinking.

Tassora asked, "You came here for a reason?"

"To warn you," he said. "The Day People plan to ambush you at the pass. I thwarted their plans, maybe. Or postponed them, but I think they'll still come."

Tassora looked at Casia, who had closed her eyes.

"Thank you for warning us," said Tassora. "We did know of their plan."

"How?" he asked, his face wrinkling up.

"We are, as you have said, 'in charge'. How exactly did you thwart their plans? And when?" asked Tassora.

"The night before last I set fire to the village. They're awful people. Small minded and mean. They deserved it. Now they'll be scrounging for cover and food for everyone. I don't know if they'll ambush you or not."

Hypatia reeled at his words. The people of his village might have been small minded and mean, but he was a monster.

"Will they know it was you?" asked Tassora.

"Yes. I made no attempt to hide it. And I've disappeared," he said, his face beaming.

Casia said, her eyes closed, "And I see you set fire to your house first so no one would be alive to confirm your disappearance."

His jaw clenched and he said nothing.

Tassora looked at Casia again.

Her eyes were open this time. She shook her head.

"They're furious. Several people died. They're coming to the pass. For him," Casia said, pointing to Tavor.

He flinched.

Tassora gave a deep sigh and looked down.

Finally, she said, "We will need to think about this. You are Moon People, at least half, your eyes claim you as one of ours. We do not normally give up our own. Yet you have committed a horrific crime against the Day People. Even if they tortured you, none of them killed you. I cannot say if your actions are justified, but what you have done mades it very difficult to defend you."

Tassora turned to Amuna. "Take him to get some food and help him find a place to sleep."

She turned back to the boy, "We will be flexible in our decision, because you are so young and because you have been treated badly by the Day People. When we decide what should happen to you, it will be with the end of making you a whole person again. In the meantime, the hunters will stay with you. Once we've made a decision, you will be given the chance to accept it, or leave us to go where you will. Do you understand?"

Relief flooded the boy's face. He really was so young. And terribly afraid, behind his bravado, Hypatia saw.

"Yes. I understand," he said.

"Good, now go get food, water and rest. We leave at dusk," Tassora said.

Amuna untied him and motioned for him to come. She walked away.

When he followed Amuna to the other edge of the camp, Tassora said to Hypatia and the other women, "Every choice that I can see to make here has problems. I will sleep on this and you should too. We'll need to decide at the pass tomorrow night. Rest well."

Hypatia laid out her furs, ate and wished Raven was here now. Perhaps he'd have some wisdom to impart. But he'd gone to stretch his wings.

She fell asleep, her mind filled with questions that had no answers.

CHAPTER 8 - TAVOR

TAVOR SAT ON A BED OF FURS, CHEWING ON DRIED OUT mountain goat meat. It tasted like it was a day or so old.

The Moon People were moving up the mountain side now. The stringy grasses and scratchy brush of the plains was below them. They were surrounded by a few pungent smelling evergreens, not closely enough spaced to really call it a forest. And the trees up here were short and windblown. He didn't know what type they were. But soon, they'd be above even the tree line, where not much grew except rocks.

The pass wasn't much farther past that. Still, he'd seen no signs of Mase or his men.

He didn't understand the Moon People. He'd come unprepared to meet them and felt stupid.

The old women had treated him kindly considering he'd made the Day People more angry than usual. No, that was underplaying it. He'd probably just started a war.

The meat tasted good despite being charred on the outside. And there was some sort of roasted root he'd never eaten before. It was sweet and earthy tasting.

The hunter who'd brought him in, sat next to him. She was eating as well.

How could a woman be a hunter? That would never happen among the Day People. Women had their roles and men had theirs. Hunting was not something a woman should do.

But things seemed different here. His judgement was put up in front of old women. They would decide his fate. Were they actually in charge? Why was that?

It probably didn't matter. They were all going to die in the war anyway. Would the old women lead them into battle? Then they'd lose for sure.

Who would be leading the Day People? Who was still alive?

He wasn't sorry if he killed any of them. None of them had even liked him, let alone cared if he was dead or alive. And why should they? He'd always been worthless and sneaky and a horrible person.

Hatred roiled around inside his belly, spoiling his pleasure in the food. He didn't deserve to enjoy it anyway. He hated everyone he'd ever known. And he didn't like any of these Moon People either.

Which one of them was his father? The man probably didn't even know about him. It wasn't like he'd ever come back and checked on Mom.

Why would he? Then he'd have to claim any child he'd made.

And who would want to claim him? A worthless pile of crap like him?

Tavor ate more meat.

"You should finish eating," said the hunter. "You'll need to sleep before we move on tonight."

He nodded.

Why had he come?
What sort of welcome had he been expecting anyway?

CHAPTER 9 - HYPATIA

HYPATIA ROSE RELUCTANTLY FROM THE PILE OF SOFT FURS. IT was still daylight, although the days up here in the mountains weren't as warm as down below. She kept her fur wrapped around her shoulders.

There was no fire for cooking breakfast, although smoke still formed a tiny spiral up into the sky, leftover from the morning's fire. She found some dried meat and a few berries someone had picked. They were chewy and unpleasantly tart, but she ate them anyway.

Tonight was the night.

They'd climb to the pass and confront the Day People.

Casia had confirmed it again this morning. Nothing had changed except the level of the Day People's anger.

Hypatia stood and rubbed her face, feeling the rough, peeling skin. Her stomach felt upset. She knew the feeling well. Anxiety. She was scared.

Mala smiled and waved at her. The woman had been very busy most days, making sure her son stayed out of trouble and didn't re-injure his arm. Her partner, Amuna, was too busy on the trek to watch him. She needed to be a hunter and now, a guard.

So, Hypatia hadn't spoken much with Mala, only a nod or smile. Hypatia missed the woman's calm ease and confidence.

She could really use more confidence tonight.

Raven dove out of the sky and landed on her shoulder, his wings whirring.

'Well, good morning,' she thought to him, startled.

'Good morning, time to eat?'

Hypatia walked towards the nearly extinct fire and pulled more meat off the carcass and handed a sliver to Raven. She put the rest in her mouth.

Others had begun to stir in their furs.

Were they also trying to find enough courage to face the dusk? She didn't think an announcement had been made, but everyone knew a confrontation was coming.

The appearance of the boy had raised questions. Apparently, it wasn't an uncommon thing for half bloods to appear. Sometimes the mother was a Moon Person and sometimes a Day Person. Eventually, when the child came of age, they sorted themselves out and joined with the group who suited their needs best.

Having such large eyes, designed for living at night made seeing during the bright day light painful, she'd been told. And not being as strong as everyone else and having poor night vision was difficult. She could attest to that.

As soon as Sian, Casia, Tassora and the others were up, everything started.

The boy was taken to have his head shaved, so he looked like the other boys his age. He was dressed in clothes that looked like theirs.

Tassora hadn't told anyone her plan, so Hypatia watched with curiosity.

Apparently, on some level, he'd been accepted by the group. She also notice that Amuna never let him out of her sight.

The boy's clothes and pack were burned. He was given a pile of furs to wrap his spare new clothes in and to wear as a backpack. She would never have noticed him in the crowd. He looked like all the other boys.

Everyone packed up and moved out. The climb was steeper today. There would be no cover since they were leaving the stubbly scrub trees behind. This high up in the mountains was an arid climate. The moons rose as the sun set. The red, salmon and orange colors in the sky looked glorious.

People were quiet. They never made much noise anyway, while traveling at least. They walked softly and spoke little.

Tonight was mostly silence.

Hypatia stayed near Tassora and the others. They'd need to be together when the time came. She noticed that the bulk of the hunters and warriors hadn't traveled on ahead as normal. Tonight they were scattered throughout the group, but most heavily around the old women.

This would never have happened on Earth. Old women were at the bottom of the food chain. Among the Moon People, they were at the top. She still hadn't adjusted to being honored. To people treating her as if she had something to add.

The air felt fresh and cool. As they switched back, she caught a different scent. It smelled faintly like the sea. The party stopped momentarily, as if to breathe it in.

How close were they to the summer camp?

Then she noticed people silhouetted on the ridge tip against the moonlit sky. She elbowed the hunter next to her and when the man looked at her, Hypatia inclined her head towards them.

He nodded. So he'd already seen them.

People kept moving forward. The trail had switchbacks, but

still people were trickled far down the slope because the trail was only wide enough to walk six abreast.

"When we get up near the top, there's a wide flat area," said Sian.

Hypatia nodded and kept walking.

Suddenly Tassora began singing in a deep voice. Chanting really, it reminded Hypatia of waulking music from Scotland that she'd heard once. The rest of the people began singing along as the song made its way up and down the line. The valley they were climbing out of echoed with the sound of so many voices, increasing the volume. Hypatia couldn't quite catch the words, but she hummed along with the melody once she found it.

They continued climbing upwards. The other old women took her hands and they began to ground themselves. Going through the process Tassora had taught her of visualizing herself as a tree, connected to the earth beneath them.

Hypatia felt the power surge between herself and the other old women and as they moved onto the high meadow and into the center. She knew they were ready.

The moons were high in the sky and the meadow was completely lit. Even the Day People could see.

She heard Casia suck in her breath. "There are more than I expected."

"Everything will be fine," said Tassora. "Just hold the circle. No matter what happens."

The movement forward stopped.

They stood still at the center of the Moon People, surrounded by warriors and hunters. The hunters and warriors had drawn ash and charcoal designs on their skin and hair. The black and gray-white swirls, stripes and other shapes looked especially menacing in the moonlight.

Hypatia settled into a state of acute awareness, holding the circle and observing the world.

The Day People were all men. They wore woven clothes, pants, tunics and big, heavy boots. Most of them held a sword or a bow. Some wore knives at their hips. And they had beards. It was then that she realized the men of the Moon People didn't have beards. Or facial hair at all. No eyebrows or eyelashes. Just some hair on the top of their heads. Which they frequently shaved off.

The Day People's faces were a mix of anger, fear, hesitation and waiting.

The Moon People's song had dwindled out.

Tassora said, "Welcome brothers. Why do you meet us here?"

"We do not need to speak to you grandmother. And we are not your brothers. Who is your leader?" asked one of the men, sneering at her.

One of the more horrifying looking guards snarled, "Our leaders are the elders. We are led by wisdom, not youth."

Tassora patted the guard on the shoulder and Hypatia heard her whisper, "Not yet."

Tassora stepped farther forward and said, "I did not mean to insult you by calling you brother. We share the same air, the water and soil. To me you are a brother. I can understand that you may think differently. I am Tassora and I speak for our leaders tonight. What would you have me tell them?" she asked firmly, but kindly.

"We seek a boy. He was born to one of ours, his father a Moon Person. He killed many of us a few nights ago and fled," said the big, burly man.

"We have seen no such stranger," said Tassora.

Hypatia wondered where in the group the boy was hidden.

He was probably painted like the hunters and guards. All the young boys she'd seen had painted themselves.

"We have too often been lied to by Moon People to believe you," the man said, in a growling voice.

Hypatia could feel the tension surrounding her in the air. Not from the old women, but from everyone else. The Day People were posturing aggressively. The hunters and warriors responding. Everyone else looked afraid.

"What sort of lies have you been told by Moon People?" Tassora asked, her face wrinkled with curiosity.

The man shifted his weight as if uncomfortable and said, "I can't remember the exact words, but it's happened. Too many times. Mostly, it's your stealing we hate."

"Stealing?" Tassora asked.

"Yes. Grain, swords, clothes, food. Stealing," he bellowed.

"Our people have always traded with the Day People. In exchange we've given rare and healing herbs, roots from the forest, berries, deer, elk and bear meat. How is that stealing?" she asked, her hands on her hips."

"We do not want your goods," he said.

"Well, thank you for finally telling us. Our trade agreement can end, if you wish, but do not ask to renew it when the choking sickness takes all your babies and you have no herbs to heal them. Or when your cows all eat the blue flame flower and die and you don't have enough meat to survive the winter."

"We will not, you can be sure of that," he said, looking around at his friends.

"Good, it is pleasing to know you can care for yourselves. What we give are things for survival. What you trade us in return are things that make life a little easier. They are not necessary. We can live without them. It is sad to end a partnership which has lasted for many generations and was helpful to both, but so be it," she said, shrugging her shoulders, her hands up.

"So, all the Moon People will leave us alone?" he asked.

"There are four other groups who probably pass through the plains, which is, I assume, where you live. I cannot speak for them. When we meet in late summer, I will convey your wishes. Whether they will agree will be decided by them."

"Then talking to you was useless," he said, looking at the other men he came with.

"We will honor your wishes. I don't believe speaking to each other is ever useless. We never knew you didn't want the food and herbs we brought you," she said.

"About the boy…," he said, his body rigid.

"Like I said, we have seen no such stranger. It is possible he went to one of the other groups of Moon People. Or that he is wandering, lost. Or perhaps he is injured or dead. Why would he want to kill any of you?" she asked.

"He was crazy. And angry. He killed my boy. Set the whole village on fire. People couldn't get out of their homes and they burned to death."

"That's horrible," said Tassora. "My heart goes out to all of you. I have no words to help such a loss."

"There are no words," said the man. "There's only vengeance."

"We cannot help you with that," said Tassora. "Nor is it our place."

The Day People grumbled amongst themselves and the big man said, "We need to search among you for him."

Tassora closed her eyes for a moment, then said firmly, yet calmly, "You will do no such thing. To do so is to say we are dishonest. You will leave this mountainside immediately and not bother us again. We've been very patient with your insults, but we will not allow any more."

She was immediately surrounded by the warriors, whose weapons were out and pointed at the Day People.

Tassora moved towards the back of the warriors and rejoined the old women. She joined hands and linked into their energy, although Hypatia felt as though she hadn't left them.

The energy surged. The sky rumbled with clouds and lightening. The moonlight was blocked out and Tassora's voice became huge, deep and resonant.

"Go, young man, go now or you may not survive this night."

Hypatia felt surprised at the immensity of the energy which flowed through the old women. She hadn't ever felt anything like it. She tried to hold the circle, even out the energy and let it flow through her, like they'd practiced. The ground shook with the thunder. The sound nearly deafened her.

Was Tassora controlling the weather? Were they at risk for being hit by lightening? Or was it illusion?

There was scuffling amongst the Day People and they were given a path down the mountain and down the switchbacks, accompanied by the warriors.

It seemed to take forever for the Day People to move past them. How many were there?

At one point the big man yelled, "We'll be back. With more men. You'll see, you can't push us around."

Hypatia had the feeling he was deadly serious.

They would be back.

Her heart pounded in relief and dread.

The way ahead was clear and a few of the warriors and hunters led. They continued to climb over the ridge for what must have been an hour longer and the clouds cleared, the moons returned.

Hypatia could see the beginning of dawn. Salmon pink and even orange creeping across the horizon behind the huge cliffs. Behind them, down on the plains, the horizon turned a lovely lilac color.

When they topped the pass, Hypatia sucked in her breath at the view.

In front of them lay a vast ocean, the coast line extended both directions as far as she could see. The shore curled around into small coves and jutted out with huge rock formations which reached out into the sea. At the foot of the mountains lay miles and miles of grassy shoreline, punctuated by clumps of woodlands. Although there were places where the rocky mountains went right up to the edge of the sea as well, like right below them.

She turned and looked behind. Flat plains lay below and in the distance from which they'd come, more woods and mountains.

Her nose caught the smell of the sea, even way up here. And in the distance, she saw huge splashes in the water and many dark shapes.

"The great ones," said Tassora, nodding at the moving shapes.

They must have been the size of a supertanker. Or one of those massive cruise ships she'd seen in Puget Sound. Except there were hundreds of them. They were larger than whales, but didn't look like them at all. Occasionally, a long tentacle would reach up into the air as if stretching. The tentacles were longer than the creatures.

Hypatia just stood and stared, watching them frolic in the waves.

People passed by her and still, she stood and watched. Frozen in amazement.

After days of moving upwards, they began to go down. It was much harder, but the people behind gave everyone space to go slowly. And the old women in front were moving sluggishly.

Still, Hypatia could feel the excitement coming from behind them. The closer they got to the sea, the higher it built. When the road began to spread out near the bottom of the cliffs, people began to surge around her. Some, especially the children, ran down the road, towards the sea. Taking shortcuts and smaller paths, racing to see who would get there first. To be the first to touch the water.

Hypatia felt relief.

The Day People were behind them. At least for a while. Here the Moon People obviously lived off the sea.

"Why do you not stay here all the time?" she asked Casia.

"The winter storms are too harsh and we don't want to use up all the fish and shell fish in the area."

Hypatia asked, "Can't you move farther up or down the coast?"

"The winter is too brutal here. The sea rises too high. The air grows too cold. There isn't enough wood anywhere here to keep us all warm and fed. That's why we've always moved back to our mountain in the forest for the winter. But the Day People breed like cassenga and come onto our lands, then complain when we want to trade with them. When I was a child, there were no Day People on the plains where we travelled from the mountain to our summer camp. Now they have scattered everywhere, led by arrogant fools," said Tassora. "There will be problems with them when we return to our mountain. We will all have to think on this and plan for it."

Hypatia nodded. "What will you do with the boy?"

"He has the Day People's disrespect for the elderly and for women. It seeps out of him like a disease. And he has murdered many people. I do not know, yet. I have been waiting until we are settled here for a time to see what changes he can make. But he must be dealt with. He will be shadowed by Amuna for a time. She is strong enough to gain his respect, if he's willing to give it. If not, then he has no place with us," said Tassora.

It took them until long past dawn to finish the descent. Of course the ones who ran ahead had already been there for half the night. Some people had begun to make shelters using driftwood as the structural part and weaving fern fronds and small branches from a sweet smelling shrub as the wall and ceiling material. Other people just spread their furs and fell asleep after they'd walked to the sea and waded into the water.

Hypatia dropped her furs and removed her boots, following Sian's lead. She walked across the sand and waded into the water, finding it surprisingly warm.

"It is shallow here, on the sand," said Sian. She pointed to the cliffs, "Over there, it is very deep, good for fishing, but not for wading."

Raven, who'd been sitting silently on her arm the whole trip flew off into the trees in search of food.

From above, the waters had looked very murky, but down here, wading into it, Hypatia could see brightly colored, small round rocks and clumps of seaweed waving in the tide. She could have waded all day long, the water felt wonderful on her tired, sore feet. Except that she was exhausted. And she knew that all that walking downhill would have her muscles aching when she woke. They ached now.

She walked back to her furs, sand stuck to her feet and ankles. She laid down on the furs on the soft sand, not even bothering to wipe off her feet or wonder about dinner. She pulled a fur over her head to block out the sunlight and fell fast asleep.

Hypatia woke as the sun was setting. The land and sea glowed golden for a few minutes and then it was dark. The moons had barely risen. The cook fires had been started and it seemed only a few people were already up, harvesting shellfish and other things that Hypatia had no idea what they were. Fat slug-like things that came from the ocean. She really didn't want to eat those.

She wandered through the camp watching people make shelters, weave reeds and prepare food. A group had found a newly fallen evergreen, she could see the wood was still green. They were scraping the inside of the log out with sharp rocks and knives.

"What are you doing?" she asked.

"Making a boat," said one of the women. "To catch fish."

She nodded and walked on. Hypatia realized that asking other people a question she felt curious about never happened in her old life. She'd changed since coming to this world. She never wanted to go back to her old life. Although sometimes she missed the books and the comforts, here she felt alive. And she could talk to people.

Still, she felt uneasy. She worried about the confrontation with the Day People. They would come back. And they'd bring more people. Flash and magic might not work to scare them off next time.

And the boy? Had he really killed all those people? Had he done it on purpose or was it an accident? Would he just cause trouble here?

She shook her head and walked on.

What was she doing here? She had no real purpose. The Moon People seemed to view her as an elder, but the others all had a skill. Sian made dyes and wove clothing. Casia painted. Solia was a herbalist and healer, Quinna was a storyteller and keeper of the tales and Tassora was quite simply, wise. She always had an answer.

Raven dropped down from the sky onto her shoulder.

She'd taken to wearing the fur on it whenever she was awake. There was no telling when he would show up.

The bird cackled at her, "Second thoughts, heh?"

"About what?"

"About the work I gave you to do."

"The Moon People already have a story teller, why is it important for me to write things down," she asked it.

The bird fluttered its wings and let out a soft sound which reminded her of a sigh.

"So people don't forget. Quinna will die. You will die. It's important that the wisdom and stories live on. This world is changing. The young people need to be taught, so they will remember. You will be their teacher."

"I can't do this. I'm not a teacher. I don't know enough."

"You know enough to teach the youngest ones. Start with them. Gather the young children and tell them stories. Show them how to write. And you write all the stories down, so others can read them."

"I don't know how to be with children. I don't understand kids."

Raven squawked, "Weren't you a child once? Go back to then. Watch the children, see how they learn, talk and think. Observe. You must learn how to do this. Begin now!"

Raven flew off into the trees and started all the birds in the woodland cackling and twittering.

Hypatia took a deep breath.

She knew Raven was right.

Hypatia needed more supplies if she was going to teach the children how to write. Casia had given her a few sheets of the coarse paper made from reeds and some thin paint several afternoons back, while they were still traveling. Hypatia had sharpened a small stick and written down a couple of the stories Quinna told her.

Quinna had no end of stories and Hypatia knew that writing down all those stories would take her months, if not years.

She kept walking down the beach, marveling at the great variety of shelters people were making. Some were woven with fragile ferns, others with glossy branches from shrubs in the woodland and these were threaded with a swamp-like grass which grew everywhere. The one in front of her was the largest building so far. The entire community could probably crowd inside. She peered into the interior and could smell a sweet scent. It was coming from the grass.

The interior was cool and dark. Easier for the Moon People to see in the daytime. Now, the moonlight shone in. The building had large doors on all sides, so it could open to the summer breezes and be shut to block out the light, she guessed. Thankfully, the nasty flies which had plagued them during the day on the plains seemed absent here.

She liked getting up before most everyone else.

The solitude felt comforting and she missed living in daylight. Her night vision was okay, the moons were bright and one, the yellowish one always seemed to be full. The blue green moon seemed to wax and wane. What effect would that have on the tides? Would they be more stable with one full moon all the time or would the blue green moon take precedence and make high and low tides? Her mind whirled with questions and plans.

She needed to have Casia show her how to make paper from the reeds. And how to make more ink. And she needed to sit and listen to Quinna more.

Hypatia wanted to help. Wanted to be a part of this community. Wanted to be a part of something, for the first time in her life.

Better late than never.

CHAPTER 10 - TAVOR

Tavor stood knee deep in the cool, salty water, his feet growing numb. His fingers raw from the wet work, he sawed at another clump of fishy smelling reeds with the dull knife. They didn't trust him enough to give him a sharp one probably.

He didn't understand these people. Everything about them was so strange. Their clothes, their food, their customs. Even though his eyes saw better at night and the blood of the Moon People flowed through his veins, he didn't feel at home.

It was hard to get used to going to bed when the sun came up and waking when it set. They'd shaved his head so he'd look like all the kids his age. Long hair was for elders they told him. He could grow his hair when he'd accomplished things.

What things?

They were teaching him baby stuff. And women stuff. How to cook, how to be clean, manners. He didn't want to know any of it.

And that woman, Amuna, was always watching him. Except when he slept, then there was a man, Jako, who with him. Jako was a half blood, like him, and apparently didn't mind being awake during the daytime. This whole place felt backwards.

This morning, actually afternoon, he and Jako were cutting down large reeds. The round stalks were to be made into paper so they had to be cut close to the ground. They grew in swampy sea water and it was hard to make his way into the thicket.

His feet were freezing numb and he still wasn't used to going bare foot. His skin was blistered and bruised from the abuse. At least there weren't rocks where the plants grew. But there were little pinching crabs that lived between the plants. And those bastards hurt, so he'd learned to step carefully, waiting for them to get out of the way.

The sun blazed down on his bare head and he knew the sunburn would only get worse. The Moon People probably never had sunburns on their shaved heads. They slept all day. Jako had hair down past his shoulders, so he wasn't getting burnt on his head at least.

Tavor cut more stalks with his dull knife. It *was* possible the Moon People couldn't sharpen the knife.

But if they didn't trust him, could he blame them?

He was a murderer. No matter if the Day People deserved it or not, he'd murdered some of them. Jase had died. At least that's what Mase said up on the pass. He'd deserved it.

But how many others had he killed?

He felt shame about that. It hadn't been a clean kill either, like in a fight. He'd taken the coward's way, killing by setting buildings on fire when people were sleeping.

And then he'd run.

So, how was this better than living with the Day People? He was grubbing around in a swamp instead of amongst the vegetables.

The Moon People treated him better. They didn't beat him

like his mother's husband had. They didn't trust him, but they at least didn't hurt him.

He sheathed the knife and gathered the armload of stalks he'd cut and carried them out to pile them with the others.

Tavor wiped his head with his shirt and looked at Jako.

"We'll need more," the man said. "It takes a lot to make paper."

Tavor carefully waded back into the center of the thicket, watching out for crabs.

"Why is it that the people who rule here are women?" he asked Jako as they worked.

"Our elders have always ruled. They are not always women. But our men often die younger than women."

"So, if there was an old man he would rule?" asked Tavor.

"The elders rule together. They must agree for anything to change. It makes our people solid."

Tavor shook his head. It was a strange way for things to work. Among the Day People one man was in charge. He'd listen to the opinions of other men, but he made the final decision.

"I know it is not the way of the Day People, but it makes us stronger, I think. Among the Day People I was born to, there was always much arguing and even killing to be the person in power. And if that person didn't care about others, his rule was awful. And anyone who was helpless, women, children, people who were crippled or hurt, they were abused."

"It was that way in the village I lived in," said Tavor.

"Here we treat everyone well. Even those who can no longer be as helpful as others. Everyone can do something and they need to be useful," said Jako.

Tavor mulled over what Jako had said, as he cut more armfuls of stalks. He'd hated the Day People and their meanness. Perhaps it was better to be ruled by old women.

Would it be better though when the Day People came again and attacked them? He wasn't sure. Mase was a fighter, not a true warrior like some of the Moon People, but he was scrappy. Tavor didn't want to meet him in a fight. Mase would gather together the other villages and Tavor wasn't sure the Moon People would be on the winning side. Despite all their strengths. The Day People would attack during daylight next time, with a huge force.

And with steel.

The Moon People didn't have that many swords. They used bows and arrows much more. So they'd be better at distance fighting. But Tavor was thinking Mase wouldn't let it come to that. Mase was tricky.

He'd prepare an ambush somewhere the Moon People wouldn't be expecting it. Somewhere where the fighting was close and the Moon People wouldn't have an advantage.

Tavor should warn them. Who could he tell?

CHAPTER 11 - HYPATIA

HYPATIA SAT ON THE SANDY BEACH. RAVEN SAT ON A NEARBY log, his feathers fluffed out, his eyes closed. The sun had just set and the Moon People's day had begun. She'd been up for hours, writing down stories and felt tired now.

She chewed on a crunchy piece of cooked fish, one whose name she had no idea of. But it tasted good.

Unlike last night's catch.

That awful fish flavor had still been in her mouth when Quinna had gathered people around and they sat, listening to the day's story. Some people wove, others scraped tree bark and others just sat.

Hypatia had sat in a row just behind the children. She wanted to watch their reactions to the story.

"It was a cold night, the moons' light was almost hidden behind the clouds. Eesia was just a thin curve in the sky anyway, but golden Ananna, she was her full self, giving the people just the right light to see by. Not too hot like the burning Shamar.

Winter was coming. The people were packing up to leave for their winter camp. Mothers shivered in their furs, keeping their children beneath the furs also. Ice was forming on water skins. The cold winds and fierce storms wouldn't let them live by the sea. But there were so many of them. The people had been happy and their numbers had grown. No longer could they all fit inside the mountain.

They trekked over the pass, still unsure what to do. Then they spread out on the plains, still without any guidance. One night Tellenia, who was the eldest of all, she stayed up long past everyone, long past Shamar's golden gleams covered the land. She walked far from the camp to be alone and sat on those flat, barren plains.

And who do you think should come to talk to her?"

Quinna looked at the children as if asking them the question.

For a while no one spoke, then one child said, "Mouse?"

"No, not mouse, although that's a good guess."

"Deer?" said another.

"No, another good guess."

"Raven?" said a third, glancing at Hypatia.

"No, another fine choice. No, it was Blood fly."

"Eeew," said the children.

"Blood fly came and sat on her boot. He asked, 'why are you troubled Old One?'

And Tellina replied, 'We have become so many, we will no longer fit inside our safe home. I do not know what to tell our people.'

'You must tell them to split up. That's what we flies do when our homes become too small. The youngest families must begin a new home.'

'But do you not miss them?'

'Of course we do. But we know there is enough food for everyone that way. We can all live. We come together at mating time. We gather and find new mates as is our custom. It keeps us strong. Then we separate again until the next mating time.'

Tellina folded her hands and said, 'Thank you brother blood fly for your wisdom.'

And that is what Tellina and the other elders decided to do.

So, to this day, we Moon People come together in the fall, on our journeys to our winter camps. We meet for a few weeks to renew friendships, find mates and then we go our separate ways again.

Hypatia watched the children's faces light up.

"Do we play games?" asked one.

"Yes," said Quinna. "It is a time of feasting, of game playing and of trading. It is a celebration."

The excitement of the children was palpable. They couldn't sit still any longer. Each one looked ready to jump up and go practice their skill at racing, or jumping or go make something to trade.

She happened to glance at the new boy, Tavor, that was his name. His face looked shocked. No horrified. As if he'd just heard something awful.

She'd only spoken with him once. Perhaps she should do so again.

What did that look mean?

After the lesson, she went to visit Tassora.

Tassora had been sick ever since they'd come down from the pass. When Hypatia asked her what was wrong, she only said, "Using magic such as I did, it takes something away from one. It was powerful magic and it was worth it to delay that confrontation, but the next one will be worse," she said. "You must be the one to record what has happened. And join with the other elders to prepare for the next confrontation. You will not get out of it so easily. The Day People have grown far stronger than we realized. They have never before been a threat to us."

Hypatia nodded, smelling the pungent scent of taisha root. Solia had told Hypatia that she made it for Tassora to ease her way.

The old woman had gone from a vital old woman to a

wrinkled shell covering bones in just a few weeks. Her skin had become translucent and gray. Hypatia knew she must be dying and wanted to stop it.

Tassora told her, "You cannot stop the world, my dear. I am at the end of this journey. I will die here and be lifted into the sea. I shall travel to other worlds and see what lies on the other side of this great ocean. I have lived a long life and a good life. I am ready."

Hypatia nodded.

"Tell our elders to contact the other groups, now. Tell them about the Day People. You must all be ready. The hunters and warriors must begin training hard. You cannot avoid this. You must take the lead here. The other elders are not strong enough to carry this much power."

Tassora gave Hypatia her necklace, made of the jet black beads which had been carved from polished stones. Pieces of the nearby cliffs.

"Take this. It is yours now. When you are finished with it, you will find someone to pass it on to."

Then Tassora passed into another world, leaving her dead body behind.

Hypatia's heart wrenched. Pain and fear filled her gut. She sat crying for a long time. Feeling lost. She'd felt a connection to Tassora, the first in a lifetime of not caring for anyone else. And now Tassora was gone.

She left the tent, still holding the necklace and went to sit on the sand by the sea. Watching the tide go out and feeling it come in again, wetting her toes.

She wept for the rest of the night, still sitting there when the sun rose.

She looked around and saw the entire group of Moon People sitting behind her, the old women directly behind and the rest farther back. They were all weeping as well.

Solia, the healer said, "Put on the necklace and let us take Tassora to the sea. To continue her journey."

Hypatia nodded.

She pulled the necklace on over her head, arranged it around her neck and stood. Everyone else stood.

She looked at Quinna. Was she supposed to say something? Make the funeral happen?

Four people arrived carrying Tassora's body on a small raft, although it could not have taken that many to lift her. She must have weighed next to nothing.

They walked through the crowd and out into the sea. And kept walking until the water was up to their necks. Then they began swimming. They swam until they were just small dots on the water, then they must have let her go and headed back to shore.

"Look," said someone from behind her.

"The Great Ones," said another. "They've come to join Tassora on her journey."

In the distance, Hypatia saw them approach Tassora's body. The dark shapes seemed to push her along in front of them until they all disappeared far out at sea.

"It was a good death," said Solia. "May we each die as peacefully."

"May we live as vibrantly," said Casia.

Hypatia had no words.

CHAPTER 12 - TAVOR

Tavor watched the ceremony for the elder silently. The great ones terrified him. How could an animal be so large?

The woman, Tassora had stood up to Mase and made him back down. He'd never seen anyone stand up to Mase, so he had to admit he felt respect for her.

As things went on, he watched the other elders take their cue from the woman they called Hypatia. That would make her the one in charge, as much as any one of the Moon People were in charge. Except she wasn't a Moon Person. He didn't really understand quite how things worked here yet, but the elders all seemed to need to agree on something before action was taken.

He'd watched Hypatia. She always rose early, she didn't have Moon People's eyes and didn't seem bothered by the sun. As far as he could tell she spent all her time talking to that raven, watching everyone else and writing. He hadn't seen any of the other Moon People write.

But she didn't seem like the Day People he knew either. She

was just different. She acted childlike, everything seemed new to her.

She was the one he needed to talk to about the Day People. He knew where they'd attack now. And when.

He could help the Moon People prepare for the ambush.

He waited throughout the long ceremony. He waited through the feast afterwards where people sat telling stories about Tassora and laughing and weeping. He waited while everyone slept again.

Then, that next afternoon, everyone seemed to have business with Hypatia. She spent a long time sitting and talking with the other elders.

Tavor sat nearby unrolling the stalks of the plants he and Jako had cut. Flattening them into paper, pressing them with large flat rocks.

There was a lot of discussion about her not wanting to be a leader and them saying that of course she should be. That Tassora had chosen her as the one who could see from outside. The one who was better at planning. Hypatia said she didn't know enough. They said she did.

She finally consented.

Then everyone slept again, including him.

Finally two nights after the ceremony, he got up early when the sun was still up. He found Hypatia walking the beach alone. Jako followed him.

"Excuse me," he said.

"Tavor, Jako, good evening."

"I think I know where the Day People will attack us."

"Oh?" she said, her eyebrows raised.

"It will be in the fall. When all the groups of Moon People meet before they go to the winter camps."

"Why then?" she asked him.

"It's out on the plains, but in a place surrounded by woods.

They can use the woods for cover to attack. They can't let you see them from a distance, they have only knives and swords. You use spears and bows and arrows, you have the advantage at a distance. Very few Day People are skilled with bows and arrows. They've always looked down on them as Moon People's weapons. And they'll have all the Moon People together. With all the Day People together, the Moon People will be outnumbered. Probably."

"How do you know this is what they'll do?" she asked.

"I know Mase, he's ruthless. It's what he'll try to do. I don't know if all the Day People will come. But he hates the Moon People. He'd like us all to be gone from this world. It's what I would do, if I were him."

She looked at Jako.

He nodded and said, "I think Tavor is right. It's a perfect solution for the Day People. It's the worst thing we could face. We need to plan on them attacking us at every point from now on, but that's the most likely place for them to do it."

Hypatia let out a deep exhalation and her shoulders sank.

"Thank you, both of you for your thoughts. We'll need to contact the other groups of Moon People and make plans. And we need to step up our training in weapons. There's much to do before fall."

She walked off and the raven flew to her shoulder. They began talking quietly.

"That was very smart of you Tavor. I think you'll make a great warrior someday," said Jako.

"Thank you," said Tavor. A stream of satisfaction flowed through him. He'd done something right. Perhaps it would make a difference. Perhaps it would save them.

For the first time in his short life he felt useful.

CHAPTER 13 - HYPATIA

HYPATIA SAT IN A CIRCLE IN THE COOL DARKNESS OF THE BIG meeting house. Pale moonlight flooded in the open walls. The scent of a pungent herb burning in an empty sea creature shell wafted over from the open doorway. On her right sat Solia and Quinna, on her left, Casia and Sian.

"I think you're right," said Casia. "I think you must go."

"But how?" asked Hypatia. She sipped room temperature herbal tea from a wooden cup. It tasted somewhat like mint. But it wasn't. The tea made her mouth feel alive, almost fizzy.

"In the past, when we've needed to talk with the other groups, we built a boat and travelled. Otherwise, the trip is too hard. Too many cliffs to scale between the camps," said Quinna.

"How long does the trip take?" asked Hypatia, worry pinching her gut.

"About two days between each of the camps. In the past there were five groups of us. Unless others have grown too large and split," said Solia.

"And you must take some of the warriors with you. Ones who are good at planning," said Solia.

"How long will it take to build the boat?" asked Hypatia.

"They've already begun," said Casia.

Hypatia looked at her, surprised.

"It's customary when the leading elder dies and a new leader is chosen, for that leader to travel to the other groups and meet with their elders. It's a sign of respect on both sides," said Casia.

"Be grateful that Tassora died when we're at our summer camps. If it were winter, you'd be walking to all the winter camps. By the time you finished it would be summer again," said Quinna.

Sian laughed at that.

Hypatia wasn't finding anything amusing today. She felt worried. About everything.

"But what if I'm needed when I'm gone?" she asked.

"That's why there are several elders," said Solia, with a quiet voice.

"You cannot carry the entire weight of our people on your shoulders," said Quinna.

"But I've got to do the things that I'm not good at. Going on a boat, when I'm afraid of the water, going to meet new people when I feel..."

"We all have weaknesses and strengths," said Solia. "When the world demands of you that you do things you're afraid of, it's asking you to strengthen the areas where you're weak. To grow."

"I don't know how much more growing I can take," said Hypatia.

"You can take as much as the world asks," said Quinna. "The other path is death. I do not think you're ready to die."

"You're right about that. I feel like I've just begun to live," said Hypatia.

"Good, then let us go see how they're progressing with the boat," said Casia.

"And gather together the warriors so you can choose who will accompany you," said Sian.

They stood, Hypatia's hips and knees hurt from sitting on the floor. They hurt a lot these days. She was trying to get more exercise, to push her body a little harder each night. She'd always been a few pounds overweight and worked standing up, even though she never exercised. She felt terribly out of shape and weak. Even after walking from the winter camp to the summer one. She wanted to get stronger and stronger and be able to keep up.

They went outside where everyone was busy. There had been a lot of fish caught in the last few days and many people were working on deboning them and drying the meat stretched between green wood screens shaped like tennis rackets. Others were steaming shellfish in wooden boxes.

The majority of people were building a boat. They were cooking a thick black liquid in wooden boxes over coal. The wood was from the iron trees which were hard and full of resin that didn't burn well. She guessed the black liquid was resin extracted from the trees. It had a pungent smell like needles from those trees.

Other people were covering the frame of the boat, which was made from the same wood and carved into a graceful boat-like shape. On top of the frame they tied on deer and goat hides. As the liquid became hot, they painted it onto the hides using branches ending in fluffy needles, covering the hides completely with the resin.

Casia went up to Aror, the man who seemed to be directing the boatbuilding.

"How many nights before the boat will be ready to journey?" she asked.

"Five, maybe six," he said.

"Thank you," she said.

"Camma, not too thick. We want it to dry quickly so we can add another layer," he said, speaking to one of the young girls who was painting the boat with the liquid.

"I'll be ready," said Hypatia, trying to sound braver than she felt. She wasn't at all sure the thing would float. And what would happen if it hit rocks?

Several people sat carving paddles out of the same type of wood.

"How many people will be coming with me?" she asked.

"There'll be you, two warriors, six paddlers. There's probably room for two more people," said Aror.

"Who else should I take?" asked Hypatia of the other old women.

"I think you should take that boy, Tavor. He has more knowledge of the day people than anyone who's come recently. And one of the hunters, his guards," said Quinna.

"I agree," said Solia. "He thinks things out well. He has a gift for planning, I believe."

"Okay," said Hypatia, taking a deep breath. She could do this.

"Let's go speak with the warriors," said Quinna.

"Thank you Aror," said Hypatia.

He nodded and went back to work painting the boat with resin.

They went around the camp, gathering the warriors together. It took quite a while. They were spread out working in different tasks. In the end two were still missing. They'd gone off to hunt deer.

The warriors crowded together on the beach and Hypatia

said, "I must go on a journey in several nights to visit the other summer camps. We must speak with them about the Day People and their threat to us. I would like to take at least two warriors with me. They should be people who can help us plan how to deal with the Day People. How to plan an attack and defend ourselves from the Day People. I wish you all to think about who would be best suited for such work."

"Tatanga," said one man. "She is the best of us all."

"And Ravelor," said another. "He has a sharpness to see the unseen."

"Amuna," said another. "She is a great warrior."

"She will not go," said one of the women. "Her birthing time is too close."

"Aah, that's right," said the one who'd volunteered Amuna's name.

"Any other ideas," asked Hypatia.

"No, Tatanga and Ravelor are the best choices," said Jako. "They are not the best warriors or hunters, but they are the best thinkers."

All of the warriors agreed.

"And I will be taking Tavor here, he knows the Day People. As Amuna cannot come, can I ask you Jako, if you will be willing to accompany us?"

"Of course," he said. "I love going out on the sea."

She felt happy someone loved it.

A fresh cool breeze blew off the water, bringing the scent of kelp to her nose as if in answer.

CHAPTER 14 - TAVOR

TAVOR SPENT HIS TIME HELPING TO PAINT THE SMELLY RESIN ON the paddles to seal them from the sea water. It was a long process. His body ached from doing the same work, day after day. Seal the wood, let the resin dry, rub sand on the paddle with a piece of bark, to smooth the wood. Then seal it again, let it dry and rub sand on it again. Then polish it with a rough moss which hung from some of the trees in the woodland. By the time he'd finished perfecting half the paddles, his hands were covered with calluses. And he thought they'd been callused before.

He felt excited about being chosen to go on the journey to the other camps. Tavor had never been chosen for anything before, he'd always been the outcast.

He knew the reason they chose him was because he had lived with the Day People and knew the men who made the threat. But he didn't care. He would be going to visit the other camps. No one here had been willing to claim him as a son. Perhaps his father had belonged to one of the other groups. Or perhaps his father was dead. But at least he had another chance to find him.

The Moon People didn't seem to be very interested in whose children belonged to whom. They seemed to care for all the children alike. If a child was hurting, the nearest adult would comfort it. It was completely unlike the Day People. If a child didn't have a father married to its mother, then it was often cast out or neglected, like him. Among the Moon People he saw no neglected children. Everyone was cared for.

Aror came to him and said, "Come. That paddle is done. It is time to take the boat out and test it. You need to learn how to paddle."

Tavor stopped rubbing moss on the last paddle and stood.

Aror gathered together the other five rowers and Jako. They slid the boat off its supports and onto the soft sand. Then towards the water. When they were up to their knees in the water, they climbed in. Each of them took a paddle from the bottom of the boat and knelt there, on soft pads of fern and sweetly fragrant moss.

Aror showed those who hadn't paddled before how to hold the paddle and make the strokes. The boat was paddled farther out into the depths. It almost bounced on the smooth waves. What would it do on stormy waves?

This boat was different than the round fishing boats the other moon people had made. This one was long and sleek. Made to slip through the waters.

Once they were out far enough, Aror had them put the paddles down and just sit on the pads facing the center of the boat.

"Our people have always had water magic. Unless you go out fishing, you've probably never used it. So, I want you to close your eyes and just sit, listening to the sea, smelling the sea and joining with the sea."

Tavor closed his eyes. He didn't really believe he had any kind of magic, but he'd try.

The waves rocked the boat gently, like a mother rocking a child. The sea supported them. The smell of salt, fish and sea weed filled his nostrils. He could hear the waves splash against the boat, the sea birds shriek and squawk as they dove for fish and chased each other. But mostly, he could hear the waves slapping at anything they touched. Boat, rocks, logs, sand.

He tasted the salt that splashed onto his face. His hands touched the smooth wooden interior of the boat, the strength of the trees which had made it.

A larger wave passed them and the boat rocked more.

"Feel the waves as they pass us," said Aror. "Feel how we can either work with the sea or against her. The water can grind rocks into sand. What chance do you have to work against the sea? Let her support us, help us. When you are rowing, pay attention to what the sea is doing. Don't bother to fight her. Instead flow with her. Now kneel and let's practice rowing."

They rowed until the moon rose high in the sky. Then took a break and ate dried fish and drank a tea made from tart herbs. The tea made his teeth feel like they'd been scraped clean. It was strange.

Then after eating, they rowed back.

By the time they reached shore, the sun was rising and Tavor's arms and back felt as if they'd never do what he wanted again. He was wobbly. He could barely help push the boat back up on the sand.

Solia the healer and her helpers rubbed oil, with bitter herbs in it, on all of them. It smelled terrible, but he could feel the heat run through his muscles, relaxing them.

Tavor decided to pass on dinner and went straight to his furs and fell asleep quickly.

They would row again tomorrow.

If he could move.

CHAPTER 15 - HYPATIA

Hypatia sat crosslegged on a floor cushion inside her small wood and sweet fern shelter, gazing out the open door at the sea splashing in the coming darkness. The cool breeze coming in off the water ruffled her hair and brought the scents of kelp and fish inside.

She had been spending most of her time with Quinna, learning more stories, especially those concerning the other groups of Moon People and any legends about the groups coming together and meeting Day People.

The Moon People's history lay in their stories. She tried to sift through them to discover what might be truth and which parts had been elaborated on throughout the generations. She wrote down everything she heard, but knew it was only a small fraction of the stories that Quinna held in her head.

She also spent time with the other old women, trying to make her magic more powerful. To make their connections stronger.

Hypatia wasn't sure how long her journey would take. And the height of summer had passed. When she returned it might be time to begin their trek back to the winter camp already. She hoped not. She dreaded the confrontation with the Day People in whatever form it might take.

So, she kept busy.

Amuna couldn't hunt anymore, her pregnancy was so far advanced she was ready to give birth any day and didn't want to go too far from camp. But she was bored and Hypatia had felt restless. And unprepared for this voyage and the return to the mountain.

She'd asked Amuna to teach her to shoot a bow and arrow. All Moon People had some skill with weapons. They'd been taught since childhood. Hypatia had none.

So each evening after breakfast, she met with Amuna who did her best to teach Hypatia the correct way to hold a bow and shoot. By the time the boat was deemed sea worthy, she could at least hit the target. Not necessarily where she was aiming for on the target, but at least the target. She was within two feet of hitting her spot on the downed log.

The evening of their departure Hypatia rolled up her stash of paper, ink and the sticks she used as pens, in her furs. She fastened it with rope the Moon People made from fibrous plant stalks. She'd stashed the bulk of her paper high up in one of the caves. In case she didn't make it back to the summer camp before they left for the mountain, Quinna had agreed to bring it with back with her. Along with the stories Hypatia had already written down.

She'd miss her tiny home here. It was small, cozy and suited her need for solitude quite nicely. She wouldn't have that on the boat.

Hypatia sighed, shouldered her bow, the quiver of arrows, picked up the roll of furs and left the now empty shelter. As she walked across the beach, Raven landed on her other shoulder, which was covered with its customary fur.

"Well, hello," she said.

"You leave tonight on your journey?"

"Yes."

"You will learn much on this trip," he said.

"I hope so. I have so much I need to know. Will you be coming?"

"I think I will. I'll fly part of the way and ride on your shoulder the rest. It's too much work to fly all the way."

"We'll only have dried meat, fish and berries to eat."

"Which is why I'll fly part of the way. Dried food makes my belly hurt."

They walked across the crowded beach to the boat. It still sat up on the sand, only the bottom third under water. Swags of evergreen boughs and ferns decorated the outsides of the boat all the way around. Woven through the boughs were branches loaded with berries.

She looked at Quinna, her eyebrows raised in question.

"They are gifts for the sea and her creatures. A blessing for your journey."

Hypatia nodded.

Solia walked around the boat, carrying a slowly burning branch from one of the evergreen trees and letting the white smoke cover the boat. She sang a song about peace, safety and new beginnings.

Hypatia breathed in the sweet smelling smoke and felt the energy around her. It felt whole. Everyone's mind was together in this endeavor, whether they stayed or were traveling. It made her feel a little less afraid.

Raven lifted off her shoulder and flew spiraling up into the sky.

Aror came to her and took her arm, helping her into the boat and showing her where to sit. He took her fur and bow and quiver, putting them on top of the already stashed dried food and other supplies.

The other members of the journey got into the boat and their belongings were similarly stored. She noticed that once the eight people picked up their paddles, there were still three paddles left. Hypatia felt relieved there were extra ones. It meant people were thinking ahead. She was the only one who was not required to paddle the entire time. Sitting, kneeling or standing at the front of the boat, her job was to look for underwater rock formations or sunken logs. Anything which might pierce the hides of the boat.

Eesia was a tiny sliver in the sky tonight, but Ananna, as always was full, casting enough light for Hypatia to see.

The sea looked calm. For now. With the journeyers in the boat, the entire group of Moon People pushed the boat out into the water, calling out wishes for peace, health, good fishing and a safe and fast journey.

It was a boisterous farewell and the boat slid through the water straight out to sea. Once far enough from the beach where the water was deep enough to avoid any large rocks, they turned and rowed with the coastline along their left side.

Hypatia found it took a great amount of concentration to continually look in front of her for obstacles in the water. There weren't that many, they were out far enough that the water was quite deep. But the passing coastline shifted from sand to rocks and back again.

Small fish huddled in schools around the passing canoe, following it and eating the tasty berries or the foliage. They were followed by larger fish which ate the smaller ones. Occasionally, one of the rowers would scoop a net through the water and catch a few fish.

"We will eat well before sleeping," said Aror.

When would that be? The night passed with the moons

moving across the sky. How far had they come? The rowers took turns resting.

She kept on looking, amazed at the diversity of life beneath the water. Fish of all shapes and colors swam beneath them. And other un-fishlike things as well. Not quite like octopi, but they looked soft, squishy and tentacle covered. Hypatia couldn't see the sea bottom. Sometimes the boat passed over forests of kelp, encrusted with shellfish and even crablike creatures. It was an amazing world down there.

After what seemed like a very long time, Aror said, "Let me take your place. You need to rest your eyes for a time."

She switched places with him. There was just enough room in the boat for her to walk, zigzagging between the rowers. So she paced back and forth a few times, stretching as she'd seen them do.

The rowers passed a water skin between them and she took only a couple of sips, not wanting to fill up her bladder.

Eventually, she knelt in Aror's place and tried to learn to paddle by watching the others. It wasn't long before her arms turned to rubber. She needed to do this now and again. To get into better shape.

"Use your entire body," said the rower behind her. Malina, that was her name. "Not just your arms. Feel the energy coming up from your legs, pulling it up from the sea which surrounds us. Feel it streaming up through your legs, your center and your chest, through your arms, into the paddle and returning to the sea."

Hypatia tried what the woman said. The energy surged through her, eager to move. It strengthened each stroke, giving it power, so she didn't have to work quite so hard.

"That's much better," said Malina.

"Thank you."

Focusing on the energy made the rowing less routine and

much more interesting. She could do this for hours. And it rested her eyes.

It seemed a very long time later, when Aror tapped her on the shoulder to switch again.

She moved back to the front and hung over the edge of the boat, looking down. Refreshed. It seemed only a couple hours later when the sun was beginning to come up that Aror asked the rowers on the left side to stop. The boat made a slow turn to the left and headed towards land. It was sandy all the way in. Everyone got out and pulled the boat high up onto the beach.

Aror assigned two rowers to collect wood to build a fire. Others picked ferns for bedding beneath furs. Others began spitting the fish caught earlier and preparing it for roasting.

"What should I do?" asked Hypatia.

"Rest. You had the hardest work of all."

She lay stretched out on her furs, eyes closed, when she heard a swoosh of wings. Raven landed beside her and perched on someone's bundle, cleaning his feathers.

Then he relaxed his neck, which shortened, closed his eyes and dozed.

It must have been a very long flight.

CHAPTER 16 - TAVOR

TAVOR LOVED BEING OUT ON THE SEA. HE'D NEVER BEEN NEAR anything larger than a small stream before. Everything about the ocean was completely new to him.

The fresh, kelp smell of the water, the taste of the salt on his lips, the sound of diving sea birds and even the burning of his muscles. He'd never worked this hard in his life, but it felt thrilling. Making the boat glide through the waves, moving ever closer to their destination.

He could do this forever. He lost himself in the rhythm of the rowing and the connection to the sea. It drained away his anger and soothed the pain which had built up since the day he was born. Here, he felt part of something. People needed him and he needed them. Everyone worked together.

At the end of the first night he'd felt exhausted from the work. He ate quickly and slept soundly. The bad dreams he'd had every night for as long as he could remember, didn't appear.

Tonight as he rowed, two massive and powerful fish swam alongside. Tavor hadn't seen this kind of fish before. They were about half as long as the boat and had blood red scales which glistened in the water. They ate the smaller fish which nibbled on the tree boughs attached to the boat. The teeth of the red fish were enormous.

Aror knelt in front of him, watched the fish warily. The man's shoulders hunched up with tension.

Aror motioned for the rowers to move the boat closer to the shore. The closer they got to shore, the slower the boat had to move. Hypatia was constantly spotting sunken logs and rocks here. So the boat had to slow to maneuver around things. The fish slowed down too, distrustful.

The gap between the fish and the boat widened.

Then the coastline curved inward and the boat turned around it. Amor's shoulders relaxed. Tavor hoped they'd lost the nasty looking red fish.

Still, they stayed close to the shore for quite a while before Amor felt safe to move to deeper water again.

By the end of the second night, they caught sight of two fishing boats and then the summer camp of other Moon People.

Those on land pointed and everyone gathered. They yelled with excitement as the boat came towards shore.

Then the crowd parted and several elders came forward to the front.

The boat slid up in the sand and he and the other rowers jumped out, pulling the boat up higher onto the shore. Some of the people from the group came out and helped until the boat sat above the tide line.

Aror helped Hypatia out of the boat. She couldn't move as fast as those who were younger.

She went up to the elders and bowed, then introduced herself.

"I'm Hypatia, an elder of the Moon People who live two nights in that direction," she said.

They bowed in return and introduced themselves. There were six of them, four women and two men. Tavor didn't catch all their names, but one of the men who talked the most was called Sanale.

Sanale said, "You must be tired after your journey. Come, shake out your tired muscles. Then spread your furs and we will bring you food. You are very welcome. We have much to speak about."

Hypatia nodded and said, "Thank you. We do need to stretch out."

Tavor watched as she and Malina walked off towards the woods for some privacy. The men in the group went towards the woods on the other side of camp. It was difficult to relieve oneself in the boat. Possible, but a little difficult, especially for women. And there was no privacy.

Afterwards the men washed up in a cold stream which ran down from the cliffs above. Then they went back to the camp and unloaded their furs from the boat and spread them in a space which one of the women indicated. They had been given places of honor, closest to the cook fires.

The food tasted slightly different from the home camp. The cooks used unusual spices. The trees which grew here were mostly the same as those of the other camp. But there were at least two types he didn't recognize.

It felt slightly warmer here. The breeze wasn't as brisk.

Tavor sat and enjoyed the food, fish unlike he'd eaten before. Aror finished first. Tavor listened to the people of this camp ask questions of him.

It seemed as if people knew others from the different camps. They'd met at the fall gatherings. Some had competed against others in the games. Others admired someone else's skill at weaving reeds or painting.

How would he ever find his father? He had no name to give them. His mother had always refused to speak about him. Said he raped her. Having spent some time among the moon people, Tavor thought that unlikely. Every man he'd met so far had the greatest respect for women. He couldn't imagine any one of them raping anyone. They even spoke of the Day People with respect. Tavor couldn't say the same of the Day People.

They'd been quite happy to damn the Moon People, especially in his presence.

No, he'd never be able to find his father amongst all these groups. Even if the man was still alive. All he'd wanted from finding his father was a sense of belonging. But, he already belonged. They'd treated him as one of theirs from the first day he arrived. Even though they put a guard on him. Jako had become a friend.

Tavor watched Hypatia speak with the elders. She was physically, a Day Person. Her eyes gave her away. Yet, she'd become an elder of the Moon People. The leading elder of the group. She belonged. She'd made her own place.

That was what he needed to do. To grow and get better at everything he was good at. He would make his own place. And do what needed to be done.

He thought he knew what that was, although he had no taste for it now. He no longer wanted to kill anyone. But he'd do whatever needed to be done to keep the Moon People, his people, safe.

He needed to talk to Hypatia alone.

CHAPTER 17 - HYPATIA

HYPATIA FELT NERVOUS WITH THE LEADERS OF THIS NEW GROUP. She was a fraud. How could she be one of the leaders of the Moon People? She wasn't a Moon Person. She wasn't even from this world.

Her belly roiled with anxiety, stomach growling.

Raven felt her anxiety and said, "You belong here, you are one of them. Stop worrying and do what you came here for.

The elders treated her with honor, everyone did. Perhaps Raven's presence helped. She ate their spicy food and exotic fruit. Talked with the elders, small talk about the people from her camp that they knew. Wondering about their health and well being. The important talk would come later, when they were alone.

This camp had subtle differences from hers. There were a couple different types of evergreens and more deciduous trees. More types of fruit growing. The fish looked different. It felt warmer here, not quite tropical though, and she tried to keep cool and drink more liquids.

What fascinated her most though, were the fire moths. The

glowing insects flew in groups, fluttering down from the tall trees and dancing around the underbrush, perhaps looking for the pollen of night blooming flowers, perhaps mating. Their bright orange glow made them look magical. She supposed that was what fireflies looked like, although she'd never seen one. They hadn't lived in her part of the world. Back on Earth.

After the meal, the sun rose ever higher in the sky. She was shown to a shelter. The vines woven into the wood frame smelled sweet and reminded her of nutmeg. Hypatia fell asleep as soon as her head touched the furs.

She woke early, as usual, and walked around in the silence. Only a couple of other people were up. Elders. Perhaps it was true of the Moon People as well, old people didn't need as much sleep.

She chewed on some of the roasted, dried meat from last night. And ate a handful of the spicy berries from one of the bowls. The greenish berries were firm, like blueberries and had a fruity flavor along with hints of cinnamon and cardamom.

Finally, all the elders were up and they went inside a cool shelter. They sat in a circle, so Hypatia took a place.

Sanale said, "I believe you have come to us to speak of other than the passing of Tassora."

"You are right," said Hypatia.

She told them what had happened up on the pass and the conversation between the Day People and Tassora. She also discussed Tavor's thoughts on the Day People, and his actions which had prompted them to come after him.

Sanale looked at the other elders and they nodded as if they understood each other without speaking.

"And you believe that they will join together and attack us."

Hypatia nodded. "We do. Even if we're wrong, we believe something must be done differently this fall. We need to keep our people safe."

The other elders nodded.

"What do you suggest?" asked Sanale.

"We think that it would be wise to gather an elder from each group together and speak. During the summer. Come to a solution and take them back to our people before the end of fall and our different journeys to the meeting place," she said.

The elders spoke, she couldn't remember their names. She'd tried.

The woman with a shaved head said, "We do need to talk. We cannot let the Day People attack us."

The fierce, hulky looking man said, "Let us attack them first. We are strong enough."

A thin, ropy woman said, "They fight amongst themselves constantly and fight against the land. She will kill them all off soon enough if they don't kill each other. We should just avoid them until they're gone."

A short, round woman who wore flowers braided into her hair said, "I agree. If we stop trading with them, stop leaving them our healing herbs, sickness will begin to claim them in large numbers. They will either change or die. It is the way of this world."

When they had all spoken, the votes were five for avoiding the Day People and one for attacking them.

"I will go with you," said Sanale. "To speak with the other elders. We should leave the night after this. Tonight we shall help you restock the boat. And while I am gone, people should catch more fish and dry them. If we must go around and avoid the meeting place, our journey to the winter camp will be longer. We must leave earlier and bring more food."

The other elders nodded and the meeting broke up.

Hypatia spent the rest of the night walking around and noticing the differences between the two camps. Different designs in basket weaving, hair styles, even their clothing which must have been taken in 'trade' from the day people. Their music sounded more melodic. Wooden flutes played a slower type of music. Even the speech of the Moon People here was a little slower, more languorous.

At dawn she went to her shelter and her furs and Raven perched, croaking, on top of the little hut. She slept.

Hypatia woke early and ate more of the spicy green berries, taking a handful of them and folding them into a large leaf to bring along. Everyone woke early and before the sun set, they were on the boat and ready to go.

Sanale proved to be an able paddler and Hypatia took her post at the front of the boat again, looking for rocks and debris in the water.

They sped along and the mist from the waves kept her face moist. For a time brilliantly striped orange and yellow fish leapt beside the front of the boat, playing in the waves it created.

Halfway through the night, Raven settled on her shoulder as she stared into the water.

"I'm tired. It's hard flying keeping up with this boat."

"Rest then," she said.

Raven slept there, then finally hopped down into the boat and settled on the pile of belongings, where it was drier.

After a time, Aror traded places with her and she rested her eyes and rowed. It felt good to move her body after so long watching.

They stopped when the sun rose and found a little cove to take shelter in. They pulled the boat high on the sand.

Hypatia stretched for a short while, ate some dried meat and two of her sweet hoarded berries and fell asleep in her furs, exhausted.

She woke that afternoon, overheated and thirsty. Drinking some water and walking around helped. She rolled up her furs and set them in the boat. Then paced along the shoreline, Raven on her shoulder.

Three more camps to visit and then back home.

And it was home.

Not like her tiny apartment in Seattle. This was a real home, with people and friends. It felt like a family should feel like.

She'd never had that before.

She ran into Sanale, who'd also woken early.

He said, "Come, sit with me on this rock. I would teach you something."

What was it that he wanted to teach her?

"Go," said Raven, inside her head. "You still have a lot to learn."

She sat down next to him on the warm, smooth stone.

"Close your eyes and calm yourself. Breath deeply so that you're in rhythm with the world."

Hypatia closed her eyes and slowed her breathing as he instructed. Feeling her breath deepen as it flowed with the movement of the nearby waves.

After a time, Sanale said, "Now, form a thought which you would like me to know. Keep it in the front of your head. Once you have done so, form a ring of energy around it, make it blaze like the fire moths' glow and send it flying straight towards me."

She formed a thought, "*I'm worried about the Day People attacking us,*" and envisioned it surrounded by the orange glow of the fire moths. Then imagined it flying towards his mind.

He sent back a thought in the same manner. "*By banding together we will be strong enough to withstand whatever comes.*"

He nodded and said, "That was perfect. Now you understand how to speak to someone without actually speaking."

"Can anyone do this?"

"Anyone who has been trained to. It does not take strong magic. Your Raven speaks to you like this I would guess."

"You're right, he does. But he is very wise. I think he's probably got quite powerful magic, although he's never shown it to me."

"I think you're probably right. Wild creatures do not doubt their abilities as we sometimes do."

"What about people who've never seen a fire moth? They don't exist in our camp."

He looked at her, his eyebrows wrinkled. "I hadn't thought of that, I thought they lived all along the coast. I would guess imagining any small, non-threatening being would work. One that's vibrant and carries a great deal of energy."

She nodded.

The others had gotten up, eaten and were now packing the boat.

Sanale and Hypatia joined them for another day. Raven flew to her before they left.

"Are you all right my friend?" she asked him.

"Yes, but with an extra rower, you are now too fast for me to keep up. I'll rest in the boat tonight," he said.

The night sped by. Again she and Aror took turns looking for obstacles in the water. The boat seemed to fly towards the next camp which they reached by the time the sky began to lighten with dawn.

The boat was pushed up on the sand and everyone got out. Raven, who had been sleeping on the supplies flew off to the nearby woods searching for food.

Hypatia's body felt stiff and wobbly. She followed the others towards the elders who were walking slowly down the beach.

Sanale reached them first and bowed, then embraced a

small, ancient wrinkled woman.

As Hypatia came upon them he said, "Deeorra, this is Hypatia. Hypatia is the head elder of the camp beyond mine. Deeorra is the head elder of these people."

Hypatia bowed and Deeorra bowed in return.

"You are welcome here. It is good for our camps to mix and trade ideas and stories."

"We need to speak with you, once we've rested a bit. I believe it should be before sleeping. Fall is coming and we need to make plans," he said.

Deeorra said, "There is food for you. Sit and eat and relax. When you are ready, we will speak."

Hypatia felt relieved that Sanale had taken the lead here. She didn't feel like she had any credibility with elders outside of the ones she knew. And she felt bone tired. Her body ached from rowing and from leaning over the bow all night.

She just wanted to sleep.

She was led to a mat beautifully woven with a complex design of three different colors of grasses or reeds. Food was brought to her. It smelled heavenly. Aror sat beside her, grinning at the food.

"The food will get spicier the farther we travel from home. But it tastes so good. The koaha they serve with it will dampen the heat," he said.

She picked up a piece of the meat and chewed on it. It tasted like coconut, tamarind and curry. The blend of flavors made her mouth explode. She swallowed and that's when the heat showed up. She picked up the gourd of koaha and sipped it. The milky juice inside cooled her throat. The wonderful smells and tastes were worth the heat though.

When everyone had finished, the elders led them to a platform, away from the main camp. They sat on it. Hypatia's muscles still ached from the night's work.

The sun was fully up now and Hypatia felt glad for the woven mat spread on a frame above the platform, shading them.

The sides were completely open and occasionally a breeze blew off the sea, cooling her.

"You are not used to this heat," said one of the elders to her. Hypatia thought her name was Meonna.

"No, it's much cooler in our camp."

Sanale and Deeorra sat down and everyone became silent.

Deeorra said, "Let us begin. What have you to tell us?"

Sanale said, "Hypatia, would you tell them what passed between Tassora and the Day People?"

Hypatia recounted the tale, adding in Tavor's thoughts about what would happen. At the end of her tale, Deeorra sighed deeply.

"We have long been afraid it would come to this. They are not a very flexible people. What do you suggest Sanale?"

"We need to have a council. We need to decide what action to take and decide if we should meet at our normal meeting place. That is why I have come along."

"You are continuing to the last two camps?" Deeorra asked.

"Yes. And I think we should leave at dusk. I feel time growing short before the camps must journey. The earth beneath my feet tells me something is wrong."

"I believe you are right. Something feels off this fall. I watch the storms over the oceans and they look as if they will arrive sooner than usual. I do not know how many more journeys I will take, but it seems this one will be different." Deeorra paused and shifted her legs. "You two should go sleep. We will decide who will come with you and be ready to travel tonight."

Hypatia got her furs from the boat and found a space to lay them out. Then she was gone. She slept heavily and had nightmares about storms filled with rain and heavy wind.

CHAPTER 18 - TAVOR

TAVOR SLEPT AS LONG AS POSSIBLE.

Finally Jako gently kicked his feet and said, "If you want to eat then get up. We leave at dusk."

Tavor slowly sat up, "What?"

"We're leaving tonight, not staying for another day. The elders feel like we're running out of time. No extra night to rest."

Tavor sighed deeply, heaved himself up, rolled up his soft furs and took them to the boat. Then he went to the cook fires and dished up a plate of the food. More spiced meat and fruit. How could breakfast be spicy? He drank some fruity koaha juice to kill the heat.

His body didn't ache at least. He could've used the day's rest, but after four nights of rowing, his body was getting used to it now. He felt stronger every day.

And the rowing helped ease the guilt of what he'd done to the Day People. For a time.

After eating, he helped pack the boat. Then they helped the elder from this camp find a place to sit. She was seated towards the back, with the supplies, but close to the side so there was a rail for her to hang on to. She was a tiny old thing who looked harmless.

But Tavor felt as if she could see deep inside his black soul. See every mean and thoughtless thing he'd ever done. And he had no doubt she knew about the fires and the people he'd killed. He tried not to look at her.

She didn't weigh much, so they were able to keep up the pace from the day before. For an elder, Sanale was still a powerful man. His rowing had added a lot of speed.

Was he using magic to help them along? More magic than Aror had taught them? Somehow, it felt like he was. Would it be an insult to ask him? Tavor couldn't see that it would be. Perhaps after they'd camped for the night and eaten, he'd ask him.

Tavor felt the old woman's eyes boring into him all night. He was the closest rower to her. After a time the raven flew from Hypatia's shoulder to the supplies. The bird perched on top of them and he and the elder had some sort of conversation.

The raven croaked and cawed at her and she cackled uproariously as if he'd told her the most wonderful joke. After a time she began telling him a story. All the stories were new to Tavor, so he listened, taking it in, while remaining deep in water magic. His strokes never faltered.

"So let me remind you of the time when the Moon People all lived together. There were no Day People back then, at least not here, not in our part of the world."

"This was before there were too many of us to fit in the mountain during the winter. We all camped at the same summer camp. The one we just left. My camp."

"We basked in the heat of summer, fire moths glowing throughout our nights. Eesia and Ananna twined their way across the sky and our peoples' magic wove through our world. Keeping us safe, healthy and filled with joy at the beauty surrounding us."

"Much like now, although our magic is diluted these nights."

"We are losing it and we don't understand why."

"Only the elders possess great power now. Back in that time, even the smallest child understood how to use power and when not to."

She continued, "Deeorra, who I am named after was head elder. She had a council of five other elders, two women and three men."

"One day we saw a boat on the horizon. It came from far out at sea. A huge blue boat, as large as the Great Ones. It had wood from tall trees growing straight up towards the sky. Instead of leaves, there was woven blue fabric, although our people had never seen fabric before, but it was woven like fabric the Day People make. Anyway, the fabric was stretched across the tree branches."

"The wind blew this boat along and the Blue People who rode in the boat had power over the wind. They were much more powerful magicians than the Moon People. We called them Blue People because everything they wore was blue, their clothing, their ornaments, they even had blue swords. They wore strips of blue fabric braided in their long, black hair. Even their leather boots had been dyed blue. Perhaps the color was their source of power, I don't know."

Deeorra coughed, drank some water and began speaking again, "We invited them to stay, because we are a hospitable people, and they were polite guests at first. They wanted to be up during the day and made noise singing their songs and practicing with their swords. We didn't sleep very well. They would take their boat out during the day and spread wide nets over the mouth of our bay. And catch all the fish, so our nets went empty. We weren't able to dry the fish we'd need for the trip back to our mountain. There were more Blue People on that huge ship, than Moon People in our entire camp."

"And what did they give us in return?"

"The choking death. It spread through our people like a shark moves through a group of sail fish. Our people died and died, until

Deeorra found that singha berries mixed with the herb paana and taken several times a day will cure the choking and save the person. By that time half our people were dead."

"Fall came and our people prayed to Ananna the constant and Eesia the ever changing for help. The elders were told to take everyone to the winter camp. So they packed up and left the Blue People to the winter storms."

"When they returned the following spring, the ship was gone, although pieces of it could be found wedged between rocks. Occasionally, they found bones of the Blue People; their heads were shaped a little differently than ours and they were much taller. And they found a few strips of blue fabric. They burned everything they could find and cast the bones back out to sea. They remade their summer camp, erasing all they could of the Blue People. Except their swords and knives. Those we kept. And we have never forgotten them."

"So when the Day People came, we never invited them in."

Tavor had never heard of any Blue People and found Deeorra's tale surprising. There was still so much about the Moon People he didn't know or understand. Had they really lost much of their magic? And why? Having come from the Day People who had no magic, he constantly felt surprised at the magic the Moon People had. He'd never imagined one could join with the sea and let it work through him to move the boat. But when he'd lived with the Day People, they'd never even mentioned the sea. Perhaps they didn't know it existed. They had such small minds, only concerned with the next harvest or if the sheep were growing.

He stopped rowing and picked up a water skin to drink, letting the now warm water moisten his mouth and slide into his empty belly. The moons were moving towards setting and the other horizon was lightening. Shamar would be blazing across the sky soon and Aror would find a place for them to stop and camp, eat and sleep.

And then the next night would bring them to the fourth camp. Perhaps his father lived in that one. The third camp had no knowledge of him. Once again, Tavor wished his mother had at least given him a name.

CHAPTER 19 - HYPATIA

IT WAS THE SECOND NIGHT OUT FROM DEEORRA'S CAMP. THE AIR felt warm. Every day they went farther from the first camp the shoreline became more tropical. Moss dripped from trees. There seemed to be more toothy swimming things and the sweet scent of rich, sensual flowers overwhelmed even the smell of kelp and fish.

The greenish clear water had been a little choppy all night. Perhaps it was just this stretch. There were also a great many large shark-like fish that glistened in the moonlight. Maybe they were sharks, they had very large mouths and big, sharp teeth. Whatever they were, the size and amount of them made Hypatia nervous.

The boat cut swiftly through the waves and she felt a huge relief when Aror spotted the next camp. If they could get going tomorrow night, then only two more nights to the final camp. The council could happen and she could be on her way back to her own camp.

Like Sanale and Deeorra, she felt a vague foreboding about the near future. She didn't have a knowledge of magic for long enough to trust the overwhelming danger bearing down on them. But combined with the others' surety, Hypatia felt a need to hurry this trip along.

To get everyone to safety.

They landed the boat and pushed it up on the sand. The people from this camp didn't rush up to help, as in the other camps.

Hypatia helped Deeorra off the boat and Raven flew to her shoulder.

Sanale bowed before the elders, who said nothing so far. No welcome, nothing. They just stared at the travelers, assessing them.

Deeorra went forward and said to a middle aged man, "Karrel, son of my son, have you no welcome for me?"

"Aah, grandmother. I wonder at your still being alive," said the man, with a snideness Hypatia had never heard in this world.

Her mouth nearly dropped open in amazement.

The man was being unspeakably rude. She nearly went back to the boat for her bow and arrows.

Then Raven took off from her shoulder, flew straight over the man, shat on his balding head and continued on towards the forest cackling like Deeorra had on the boat.

The man cursed at him and stooped, picked up a rock and threw it at Raven, but missed. Although Raven had to swerve to avoid it.

Then the man glared at Hypatia.

Hypatia looked at Sanale and Deeorra. Sanale's face was blank, emotionless and she caught a message he sent to her.

'Let Deeorra handle this. Don't do anything.'

She looked at Aror and the paddlers. They were almost bristling from the insults, but Aror was in front of them, arms crossed and looking like a rock. Solid, immoveable. The others would follow his lead.

Tension hung in the air.

Deeorra stood in front of them all. Silent and waiting.

Her grandson stared back. Hypatia looked at all the other people. There were no elders here. Not a one. No one older than thirty or so.

Where had happened to all the elders?

Then she noticed that every single man wore a knife and sword. There were only a few women and they hung towards the back, grouped together, around the cook fires. They looked afraid.

Not like the other groups where women mingled throughout the camp, many wearing weapons, being warriors or hunters. These women were segregated.

Finally, the man broke the silence, "Why are you here?" he asked, anger tinging his voice.

Deeorra replied calmly, "Tassora has passed. We bring Hypatia, the leader of the elders on her meeting journey. We brought her to present her to your elders."

Deeorra said nothing of the council.

The sun rose over the trees, blazing down on them, into the eyes of the travelers. Hypatia could see just fine though.

Karrel smiled and said, "Our elders all died last winter and on the journey here. So, we are the elders now." He extended his arms to the four men surrounding him, not a one over thirty. All armed and ready to do battle. "She is not even a Moon Person. How can she be a leader?"

Deeorra bowed and said, "Hypatia is a Moon Person inside. Tassora chose her to be leader. Well, we have presented Hypatia. We will be on our way now. We must make it to the final camp and then travel back to our own camps again. Fall is coming swiftly."

Sanale sent Hypatia another message, *'Bow and walk backwards, get on the boat.'*

Hypatia did as he said, noting that Deeorra had already walked behind her.

She got to the boat, turned and helped Deeorra on. The woman's face was filled with fury.

Sanale and the others were walking backwards towards the boat and had just gotten there when Karrel's men rushed them.

Hypatia felt a huge wave of energy pass by her and everyone who was attacking fell flat onto the earth.

Aror yelled, "Push!" and the boat heaved off the sand and into the water. The paddlers and Sanale climbed in quickly, taking up their paddles and the boat moved rapidly through the water. Raven streaked towards them, landing on the supplies.

Karrel stood on the beach screaming at them, "You'll pay for this at the meeting place, old hag."

Deeorra ignored him, seemingly concentrating on moving the boat quickly through the sunlit waters. They kept going for half the day. Hypatia could see obstacles in the water just fine and the paddlers had renewed energy after the near confrontation.

They all did their work in silence.

Finally, they found a place to camp they felt safe enough at and pulled the boat up, ate dried fish and a few berries, then slept until dusk.

Hypatia had disturbing dreams about elders being murdered in their furs. The expressions of disbelief on their faces haunted her for the next two nights.

Each night the water became rougher. On the second night rain poured down and Deeorra spent her time bailing water out of the bottom of the boat.

Once, they pulled up onto shore for a time.

Deeorra said to Hypatia and Sanale, "He murdered them. The elders. So he could be in charge. That camp has spent too much time close to the day people. They've adopted too many of their ways. We should be separate from them. I chose not to warn them of what we know. They will perish. Most of them anyway. I didn't know how to rescue the innocents," she said, sadness filling her voice.

"You did what was right. There was no way to rescue them. They are lost to us," said Sanale.

The rain stopped and they moved on, paddling past trees which looked increasing tropical to her. The leaves were bigger, the foliage lusher, the air felt more humid and hot than at her home camp.

The trees hung looped with vines, some of them bearing purple trumpet shaped flowers the sweet perfumed scent of which Hypatia could smell all the way offshore. They smelled like the cut lilies which she used to sniff while in line at the grocery store.

Finally, just before dawn, they arrived at the fifth camp. At this camp people waved and greeted them, rushing to help pull the boat up onto the sand. Hypatia felt relieved at the normal greeting.

A group of elders came down to meet them, three men and three women.

As Hypatia helped Deeorra out of the boat, another old woman ran to her and they hugged, chattering at each other.

Sanale said, "Deeorra's sister, Leeorra. She took a partner who lives in this camp."

Another old woman with piercing blue eyes approached them more slowly. "I am Tialla, head elder of this camp and I welcome you."

"I am Sanale, head elder of a camp, six nights paddling in

that direction," he said, pointing in the direction from which they'd come.

"I'm Hypatia, head elder of the farthest camp in that direction. Tassora, the former head elder has passed on to her next destination," said Hypatia.

"I'm pleased to hear of her passing, although I shall miss her and her wisdom. I am happy to meet you," Tialla bowed again. "Please, refresh yourselves in the stream and come eat with us. Tell us about your journey. It's been so long since I've been out on the sea. I miss going, but there's always much to do here."

They bathed in the fresh water, washing off the salt and sweat. But, it was so hot that by the time Hypatia dressed she was sweating again.

Then she sat with the other elders near the cook fires, even though it felt hot, and ate the spiciest food she'd ever tasted in her life. It tasted like chiles, but the food was so hot she could barely taste any other flavor. There was sweet fruity juice which cut the heat a little bit, but long after the meal ended her throat and mouth still burned.

After the meal, the elders walked the beach alone to talk.

Hypatia told them what she'd told every camp, about the confrontation, Tassora's worries and Tavor's thoughts. Deeorra added in what they'd found at the last camp.

Tialla said, "What you have told me is very troubling. I can see now that you've come not just to introduce Hypatia to us, but to meet and decide what to do about the Day People."

Sanale nodded.

"Let me dream on this problem. The sun is up, I must sleep. I'm sure all of you are tired as well. After we sleep and eat, then let us discuss what to do."

Hypatia felt both relieved and annoyed. She wanted a decision now, but felt exhausted.

Deeorra said, "I think that would be helpful. We have had a

rushed journey here and this decision will affect our children, and theirs, for many generations. We must choose wisely."

Hypatia found where her furs had been unloaded, unrolled them and fell asleep quickly.

She woke in the middle of the day to feel the earth shaking violently. She counted, one, two. She stood up, staggering and trying not to step on sleeping people. Seven, eight. It took her a few seconds to understand what was happening. Thirteen, fourteen. It was an earthquake. She'd only been in small ones back home. Twenty-one, twenty-two. Finally, the ground stopped shaking. Then she looked out at the sea. The tide had gone way, way out. Much farther than the low tide line.

It took a few more seconds to understand what was coming next.

Tsunami.

People around her were stirring. Beginning to stand up.

"Get to the cliffs!" she yelled. "Everyone run!"

Nearly the entire camp fled for the cliffs.

She helped Deeorra up. Sanale stood looking at the sea, horror gripped his face.

"She can't make it in time," he said.

"Leave me," said Deeorra.

"No," said Hypatia.

Aror was there pushing them, "To the boat, get in."

Tialla was with them, and all the rowers. They managed to get everyone in the boat.

Fear gripped Hypatia, she felt paralyzed. Waiting for the towering wave to hit.

"Hang on tight everyone. Hold on to your paddles, but don't try to use them. Trust in water magic," yelled Aror, over the roar of the incoming wave.

Hypatia didn't feel very trusting looking at the massive wave coming their way.

It must have been twenty feet tall.

She closed her eyes and felt the energy flowing through the people and the boat. She felt the flow strengthen, become firm and fluid as everyone focused on connecting to each other and to the sea.

Hypatia took a deep breath just before the wave hit. It crashed over them and the boat rolled over and over again. She held her breath until her lungs ached, slowly letting it out. Then empty, no air left, she would have gasped for air, but wouldn't let herself open her mouth.

Upright again, another quick breath and the next wave hit taking them farther inland. She tried not to think about whether they'd hit the sharp rocks. Pushing back the wall of fear, she focused on maintaining that connection, to the others, to the boat, to the sea.

The second wave retreated, pulling them out to sea. She breathed again and another wave hit them hard, through the sound, she heard wood crack, hoping it wasn't the boat.

The waves played with the boat for what felt like hours, but she knew it could only be minutes. Hypatia kept trying to catch enough breath to survive the next wave. Her lungs ached, she was soaking wet and all salt water even filled her nose.

Hypatia tried hard to keep her focus on the magic and the connection as if it were a life line that would keep herself and everyone else nearby safe. Finally, she lost consciousness.

When she woke two full moons were high in the sky. The sea was calm. Her body was wet, except for her mouth which felt crusty and dry.

She was so thirsty. The boat's frame floated, twisted and broken, the hides still intact.

Deeorra sat watching her, bright eyes flashing in the moonlight. Tialla lay unconscious, but breathing. Sanale was looking around. Aror sat staring, his mouth open wide in wonder. Tavor had the same expression on his face. Only three other rowers were there, Malina, Jako and Ravelor. The others were all missing.

And they were far out at sea, no land in sight.

It was then that Hypatia became conscious of the massive shapes surrounding them. At first she'd thought them huge boulders, that the boat had come to rest in a small cliff lined cove.

Then they moved, and shot out breaths of air and water. And opened their eyes.

They were the size of one story houses, the color of green seaweed and slimy. The creatures were so close she couldn't take in even one's entire size without turning her head. There were four of them and they supported the wrecked boat with their tentacles, while staring at the humans with their huge multiple yellow eyes.

She sent a message to Sanale, "Are they going to eat us?"

The creatures all turned a pink color.

He laughed and said, "You know they can hear you. They are the great ones. They have saved us."

He hadn't answered her question.

She watched as they turned green again.

"Did the camp make it to safety?" she asked.

"I don't know," said Tialla. "The sea has taken us far from the camp. I've asked the Great Ones to take us back. They are trying."

Hypatia stared at them. She tried to make out their forms, but even in the light of two full moons, she couldn't see them well.

Part of them was underwater and she couldn't tell how many tentacles they had, some of the long appendages were folded up, supporting the boat. Their slimy skin looked slightly mottled, sort of like camouflage, adding to her confusion. They reminded her of a cross between an octopus and a whale. Their immense bodies contained more magical power than she'd ever felt.

She'd never seen anything like them.

She hoped Raven was safe. He had probably been sleeping in a tree in the woodlands. Or hunting.

She watched the Great Ones for hours, breathing and blowing, gliding through the water. They smelled like the sea, only much more concentrated and intense. For a long time, no land was visible, the boat must have been taken very far out. She worried about her own and the other camps. Hoping they'd been alert and made it to safety. Perhaps the waves hadn't been as high farther away.

Or perhaps they'd been higher.

What had happened to all the stories she'd written down? She'd put them in one of the old caves to protect them from rain while she was gone. But the cave might not have been high enough up on the cliff.

Why was she worrying about pieces of paper when people had died?

"Land," said Aror, his voice loud against the blowing of the Great Ones.

Everyone sat up, looking.

Hypatia saw cliffs, although she didn't recognize them. She glanced at Tialla, who smiled with recognition.

As they came closer to shore, the Great Ones shifted position, the one nearest shore left and the others used their tentacles to push the remains of the boat towards the beach. Then, it probably became too shallow and the creatures let go.

The boat began to sink and everyone swam off it, towards the shore, the stronger swimmers, helping those not so strong. Aror came to help Hypatia, who had never learned to swim.

"Just relax. Let me help you," he said. "Lie flat on top of the water and kick your feet."

She did as he said and he kept her head above water, pulling her to the shallows where she could walk.

The sun was rising by the time they made it up onto the beach. It was a horrible scene. Huge logs lay tossed over the sand where structures had stood the previous night. Had it been that short a time, or had it been longer that they drifted at sea?

There was little sign that a camp had stood there. Except that people were crawling around on the logs, moving them as they could. Searching.

The people welcomed them, clearly relieved and amazed at their still being alive. Leeorra, hugged her sister.

Tialla asked her, "How many people have we lost?"

Leeorra's face sank. "Nearly forty. We're still finding people."

Tialla gave a deep sigh and shook her head. "It would have been many more if Hypatia hadn't warned us."

Someone had collected fruit from the forest. Oblong green things which resembled papayas, something Hypatia had never had the nerve to try back on Earth. These had purple, sweet and rich tasting centers with tiny crunchy seeds. She ate a whole one and it quenched her thirst and made her realize how hungry she'd been.

They worked all day, looking for bodies and building rafts to take them out to sea. The Great Ones hovered on the horizon. The sun was moving towards setting when Raven finally came to her.

"I'm happy to see you my friend. I was worried," she said.

"I found a tall tree to stay safe in. You were not so lucky."

"No, but most of us lived."

"You do not have much time. You must make a decision

about the gathering. Since you won't be able to take a boat back to the other camps, I will fly there and give them your message. It will take me a long time to reach them all and return, so make a decision tonight."

"You can do that?"

"Fly?"

"No carry a message to them for us."

"Of course. But I do not do it lightly," he said.

"I will speak to them. I know Sanale and Deeorra are worried about their people too."

Raven said, "I will go rest now. I'm happy you're safe."

He flew off high above the cliffs.

The sun was setting by the time Hypatia had rounded up Sanale, Deeorra and Tialla for a meeting. They sat on a log, facing the sea.

Tialla asked, "What do you think we should do about the Day People?"

Sanale said, "I think we should fight. All our camps have been training for battle since Hypatia came to us. The Day People have an advantage with their many swords. We have archers and a few swords. There are woods on all sides of the Gathering Place. We are woodland peoples. We fight by stealth. That is our advantage in the woodland."

Deeorra said, "While I'm tempted to say, 'let us just fade quietly into our winter camps and bypass the Gathering Place, just now I don't think that's a good plan. The Day People have been growing too bold, too aggressive. I think we must remind them that they share this world with others."

Hypatia said, "I don't know. I just don't know what the best course is. I'm a stranger to your world. My world is filled with conflicts, fighting and wars. None of which seem to ever solve anything."

Tialla closed her eyes for a few minutes and remained

silent. When she opened them, she said, "I believe Deeorra is right. We must fight, just enough to tell the Day People that we live on this land as well."

"Where should we meet?" asked Hypatia.

"There is an old trail along the coast. We used to use it to travel between summer and winter camps, until our groups grew too large and we found the inland route was faster. Tell your people to leave now and we will join up with them when they arrive. Can your raven accomplish this?" asked Tialla.

"He's told me he's willing to take messages to the camps. Will everyone know this trail?"

"If the elders are still alive, they will remember," said Tialla.

"I remember," said Deeorra. "The elders in my camp will as well."

"I remember as well," said Sanale. "Perhaps Raven can spot the trail and help people towards it if no one can find it."

"I will ask him," said Hypatia.

"The other camps must leave earlier than usual. They must leave now. The old trail is rougher and winding. It will have become overgrown after all this time and will take longer to get to our winter camps. Our group will stay fifteen more nights here. Finish putting our dead out to sea. Some must begin training for battle, those of us already skilled, must plan. Then we will set out and begin clearing the trail. We will stop before we get to the trail which leads off to the Gathering Place. All the camps must all be together by then."

Hypatia asked, "Will Karrel take that route?"

Sanale shook his head, "I don't think so. I don't think he knows about it. He's too young and all their elders are dead. Their camp may not have survived the huge waves. We cannot know."

"Perhaps Raven can tell us when he returns," said Hypatia.

"In the meantime, we must make battle plans," said Sanale.

"We must gather together all your best warriors and we can only depend on those who are here. We don't know what's happened at the other camps."

"I agree we must do that," said Tialla. "But first, we honor our dead."

The meeting broke up and Hypatia found wood for arrows and began stripping the bark off the thin branches with her small knife.

Raven found her and she relayed the decision of the elders.

"It will be many nights before I see you again," he said. "But I will do all you asked." He fluttered his wings. "Do not worry if I have not returned by the time you leave. I may have to help the others find the trail. I will come when I can."

"May the wind speed you along and the moon light your way," Hypatia said, stroking his firm, soft feathers.

He closed his beak around her finger and pressed ever so gently, then released it.

He flew up into the trees and vanished.

He'd never been gone more than a night or two since they'd met. She'd miss him.

Hypatia went back to work making sticks for arrow shafts. When the warriors for this camp were finished honoring their dead, she'd ask for help in making a bow, the points, and feathering the ends. The tsunami had taken everything.

The next few nights she spent most of her time with Malina. The huge wave had destroyed all but one of the camp's fishing boats. The oval shaped boat was made of wood and resin coated hides, much as their long one had been. Malina was used to fishing, she'd learned how as a child. They paddled out to the next cove and then cast their nets.

"Do not paddle, it frightens the fish. Let us just drift with the tides," said Malina.

Hypatia watched as Malina closed her eyes. She knew the

woman was doing some sort of magic. She could feel the energy surrounding them, but Hypatia hadn't a clue what Malina was doing. She knew better than to ask.

"We must be silent. Don't want to scare the fish."

Perhaps it was some sort of luring magic. Attracting fish to the area, or perhaps their food, so the fish would come. Whatever it was, Malina always came back with nets filled with fish. For which the entire camp was grateful. The hunters and nearly everyone else were busy building rafts for the dead.

So she sat, feeling the boat rock with the waves, cradled by the whims of the changeable sea. Even here where it was warmer than back at her camp, she could feel the nights growing cooler. The days remained warm, but the soil was drying out. It was as if the land and plant life, were diminishing, bravely trying to carry on without water, but eagerly awaiting winter and the rain-filled storms which would give them life.

The leaves had just begin to change on deciduous plants, a little yellow on this one, a little orange on that one. Some had begun to drop their leaves without changing color. Seeds ripened everywhere, some spat their seeds out towards her, others were carried on the wind twirling or floating away to their new home.

The days passed by quickly. The dead were put out to sea on their rafts. The entire camp grieved, even Hypatia who had known none of them.

Who had died back in her own camp? Faces of friends flashed in front of her, Quinna, Casia, Sian, Solia, Mala and her son Dall, Amuna and so many others? She hoped not. She mourned the loss of Tatanga and the other rowers who'd been lost when the boat broke apart. And she still mourned for Tassora.

Who would be left after they fought the Day People?

Then the village shifted their attention to the upcoming move and the battle. Meetings of warriors were held. Sanale worked on strategies with them. Jako, Tavor and Ravelor were very involved.

Hypatia stayed away from the battle planning meetings. There was little she could add.

She got some wood and one of the warriors helped her make a bow. She finished her arrows with sharp arrowheads made from stones out of the same material as the cliff faces; chipping away at them the old fashioned way and bruising her already battered fingers.

And she practiced shooting the arrows, relentlessly. Whenever she wasn't helping gather herbs and roots. Or drying fish. Making water skins from the few hides of deer or goats the hunters killed.

It would be a cold journey back to the winter camps. And many would be short of furs for the trip. She was one of them. Others needed the warmth more.

Finally, one night Tialla said, "This will be our last night here. Tomorrow we begin our journey."

Everyone began packing. Hypatia helped Malina carry the small boat up the path to the caves in the cliff face. High enough up that the winter tides wouldn't carry it away. They stored it and all the paddles which had been found intact.

Water skins were filled from the stream and handed out to people. Dried food was put into cloth and hide bags and distributed.

Hypatia slept lightly that day on her sweet smelling bed of ferns. She wouldn't have anything this soft until they got back to the mountain. Tree and shrub branches would be it.

She woke early, anxiety making her stomach roil. She couldn't go back to sleep. It would be hours until the others got up. She slipped on the soft leather boots she'd made for traveling. Others used their hides for sleeping on. She'd made boots and a quiver.

Hypatia rose, putting on her large knife and her small leather bag of belongings. Then she shouldered her quiver and picked up the bow. She walked down the beach, after peeling off some of the fish from last night's dinner, which had been sandwiched between sticks for cooking.

It would be a long night climbing up the ridge. Apparently some of the hunters had cleared part of the trail last night.

A whoosh came through the air and a black streak landed on her shoulder with a thud.

Raven!

"Hello. How are you?"

"Tired and hurting," he said.

"Why hurting?" she asked.

"Attacked by a hawk, two days ago."

"Let me see," she said. "Hop down onto that log,"

He did and she looked at the wound across his body.

"We should put some salve on this," she said, pulling open the bag tied to her waist.

She pulled out the half shell of a wassa nut covered with a large taissa leaf. She unrolled the leaf and scooped out some of the goo inside the nut. Then spread it over the wound.

"What is it?" he asked.

"It's made from several different herbs. It will clean the wound and help it heal. Just leave it alone and try not to wipe it off. I'll put more on later if you need it."

"I won't be here. I just came back to tell you that I've been to all the camps. Your camp has a hundred people coming, they left the same day I did. Sanale's camp has seventy, they've started already. Deeorra's camp has fifty and they should have begun their journey as well. I didn't speak to Karrel's camp, as you asked me not too. There are about fifty people there. They must have left after the big wave, gone over the pass and are taking the wide road to the Gathering Place."

Hypatia's heart sank.

So few people. So many must have been caught by the tsunami.

She nodded.

Then asked, "Where are you going?"

"I must go back and help them find the path through part of the forest. It's invisible to them on the ground. I told them I'd be back to help."

"Thank you," she said.

"You don't need to thank me. I'm a protector of your people. That's why I came to you and asked you to write down their stories."

"I'm not doing a great job of that, am I?"

She offered him a piece of the fish and he gulped it down.

"More important things needed to be taken care of. You will have time to do the stories when you return to the winter camp."

"Perhaps," she said.

"Well, I must go. When do you leave?"

"We start out tonight. It will take some time to clear the path after we get past the already cleared section. Hopefully, the others will catch up with us."

"I shall see you again when the last group meets you."

"I hope your flying is easy. If that wound gets worse, ask for help from one of the other camps, please."

He croaked at her and flew off into the sun.

CHAPTER 20 - TAVOR

TAVOR SLUNG THE QUIVER AND BOW OVER HIS SHOULDER AND looked back at the beach. He wouldn't miss the water. Not after the huge wave ripped the boat apart.

It had nearly killed him and everyone he knew.

And the Great Ones, even though the Moon People had great respect for them, they terrified him.

He took a deep breath of fishy smelling ocean air and began climbing the path, following a young woman and her two children. The smell of some sweet forest flower filled his nostrils, making him relax a bit as he got into the rhythm of walking up the steep trail.

He felt changed.

The Moon People seemed to value him, to take his opinions under consideration. In his old life that would never have happened. Among the Day People he'd always been an outsider. Less than a pile of manure. At least they had a use for that.

He'd told the Moon People at the battle meeting that they

should attack the Day People first. Now. When they would never expect it. Some of the warriors had agreed with him.

Others hadn't. Sanale had said that would only inflame the Day People, make them attack the Moon People harder.

Tavor had to agree with that. Mase wouldn't take an attack of the Moon People lying down.

That was why it was important to kill all of them.

In the end, the elders decided to circle around the woodlands and move in through the woods. The Day People would probably use the trees to hide in before they attacked. So the Moon People would come in behind and attack them, then disappear back into the deep woods. The Day People didn't know the woods like the Moon People did. They didn't have that sort of skill.

The people who couldn't fight would avoid the whole area, making their way to the winter camps by the old trail, to be joined later by the warriors. They'd be safe.

That was the current plan. Sanale said things might change after all the groups came together.

One of the young children in front of him, barely able to walk, slid down the slope and fell. Tavor helped him up, the child looked at him wide-eyed and hurried back up to his mother.

As the trees enveloped them Tavor felt mixed feelings. He felt hidden, but also nervous about all the dangers that might be hiding from him.

Jako told him that among their people, some chose to stay at the winter camp all year round. They didn't like the ocean. So they guarded the caves and stayed by themselves. Tavor thought he might like that when he was old enough. When they trusted him. He quite liked being alone.

They climbed for half the night before the trail leveled out and ran along a ridge which followed the coastline. Far below the sea churned.

Aror had told him that summer was ending early this year. Aror was a weather worker, but he said that even he couldn't hold back winter.

Tavor's mouth felt dry and pasty, but he didn't drink from his water skin. He prided himself on his stamina. He'd grown up among the Day People and he understood thirst. There was no guarantee of fresh water for four nights Sanale had said.

Tavor meant to make his water last.

The hunters were taking turns clearing the trail, so it was slow going. By the time they camped for the first day, Deeorra's people had caught up with them. By the second day they set up camp, Sanale's people had caught up. Two days later on the fourth day, Hypatia's people arrived.

All together there were about two hundred eighty people moving down the old trail. There were about one hundred and eighty hunters and warriors who would go to fight. The rest, including all the elders except Sanale, would travel on to the Mountain, which was apparently the winter camp of Hypatia's people. They would be accompanied by about twenty warriors.

The wave, tsunami, Hypatia had called it, had killed over six hundred the Moon People.

They held a large ceremony honoring all who had died, including those murdered in Karrel's camp. It went on for two nights.

The only ones not participating were the hunters who had traveled ahead to clear the trail for everyone. They mourned on their own.

On the eighth night the old trail turned inward towards the Mountain. Two nights later, they came to the place to split up.

They were deep in the forest here. It was completely

different from on the coast. More evergreen trees. There were two types, katellia trees and marrona trees. They were both tall, but marrona trees were bluer and the nuts were ground into a paste to make a tasty flatbread. Both the Day People and the Moon People made it. One of the few foods they both made.

The trees created a feeling of seclusion, of safety which made him feel leery. Beneath the trees grew many types of bushes which provided cover.

He'd never even been in a forest until he joined the Moon People. He didn't feel safe not being able to see everything. He wasn't sure what predators lurked in the forest. He knew about the hurracha and the big cats. But what else lay in wait?

The air here felt cooler and had an earthy smell, as if it had rained recently. Everything was lush and overflowing with vitality, with life.

Sanale stood at the head of the line and directed people towards one path or the other. Both paths were cleared for a short distance. The hunters would continue to clear the trail towards the Mountain. Those traveling towards the Gathering Place would have to rough it. To go silently through the woods.

A couple of hunters had gone on ahead a couple of days ago. They had yet to report back on whether the Day People were there.

Tavor felt anxious about the upcoming battle. He'd not used a bow and arrow for very long and wasn't as skilled as others. He wanted to be helpful in the upcoming battle, but was afraid he just wasn't good enough yet.

He moved down the barely visible trail towards the Gathering Place. Branches swatted him in the face. He heard mumbling up ahead, but felt too tired at the moment to care. He was just waiting to find out what was happening.

Finally, word was passed down the line that the two hunters were back.

The Gathering Place was still half a night's travel away. About a hundred Day People were hidden in the woods, but they weren't silent about it. They were clumsy and unskilled woodsmen. Karrel's people were camped in the meadow, they were drinking copious amounts of looloo berry wine, making music and running races. Waiting for the other camps to arrive. They clearly had no idea the Day People were there.

Mase apparently had rounded up a hundred men to help fight. He must have gone to the nearby villages. No, even that wouldn't have been enough. He must have contacted far away villages as well.

Sanale decided they should rest for the day. To be fresher when they neared the Gathering Place.

Tavor finally fell asleep on a bed of ferns, after wasting much time worrying about the upcoming battle.

The next night the hundred and eighty warriors and hunters made their way almost silently to the forest surrounding the Gathering Place. They'd divided into four groups, one for each side of the forest. It took Tavor's group half the night to make it to the far side of the forest, since they had to skirt through the edges of it.

Then they spread our farther to cover the entire side. The two warriors on either side of him, Jako and Matan were barely in sight.

Tavor stealthily made his way deeper into the forest. He could see the Day People's fire in front of him. They'd been foolish enough to make a fire?

Or was it a trap.

The men were laughing and telling jokes. He could see them drinking ale. The small cask of it sat a ways back from the fire. He shook his head at their stupidity.

Jako moved towards him, as did Matan.

There were four men around the fire, awake. Two lying down, trying to sleep, or perhaps passed out.

Jako sat on his heels behind a huge downed log.

"We'll wait," he whispered.

Matan nodded.

Eventually the men went to sleep, all except one, who sat at the fire, drinking and occasionally, stirring the fire.

The fire died down to ashes. It would be too dark for the Day People to see.

The three of them Tavor, Jako and Matan still sat, waiting, with their backs to each other.

Eventually a man came out of the woods towards the fire.

So, there had been a lookout.

He kicked one of the sleeping men who got up, rubbing his eyes. He picked up a sword and went into the woods in the same spot the other had come from. The first lookout sat down, drank a cup of ale and went to sleep in a bedroll. The man tending the fire, woke up and then crawled into a bedroll as well.

Tavor, Jako and Matan waited for a while.

"I'll take him," said Matan, in a low deep voice.

The others nodded.

Matan got up and disappeared among the trees.

Jako and Tavor waited.

They heard nothing, but after a time Matan waved at them and pointed towards the camp.

Tavor and Jako moved toward the camp. Then Matan dropped his hand and the three moved into the circle by the campfire. Their swords and knives flashed. Throats cut. The Day People didn't even make a sound louder than gurgling. They'd all had too much ale.

Tavor felt regret as he melted back into the forest. These

men had done nothing to him. It wasn't like killing the people in his village, the people who'd tortured him since he was born. These men had intended to harm, but would probably have been too drunk to carry it out.

Still, the three of them moved forward in search of more victims.

CHAPTER 21 - HYPATIA

Hypatia walked along the trail with Raven dozing on her shoulder. He'd had a long journey flying between the camps for the last several days.

The trail wasn't as overgrown here. It was wide enough for two people to walk abreast. Perhaps one of the groups still used it every fall to travel to their winter camp.

Tall trees, both deciduous and evergreen reached towards the sky. There wasn't a lot of undergrowth, most everything had been shaded out here. The cool forest floor was littered with downed logs nursing a few small bushes and baby trees. Ferns grew here and there and moss seemed to coat everything. The air felt moist and smelled earthy.

Small yellow birds flitted between the trees, their calls melodic and strong.

Most of the hunters had gone with Sanale. At least they knew how to use weapons. Hypatia missed them, longing to eat something other than dried fish and whatever berries they happened across.

She hadn't liked Sanale's plan. Something felt terribly

wrong about it. The farther she walked from where the group had split, the more it felt like a really bad decision.

Halfway through the night, they stopped to rest. She went to sit next to Deeorra and Tialla.

"I don't like this. It's all wrong. We should be making peace with the Day People, not attacking them from behind," she said.

Tialla looked at her, as if weighing her words.

Deeorra said, "I think you are right. It's the way the Day People would act. Sneaking up from behind. It is not honest. And we are an honest people."

Tialla said, "I agree with you. I think we should turn back. Go to the Gathering Place and try to reason with them."

Hypatia asked, "Will they reason with us? Or kill us?"

Tialla said, "I've lived a very long life. The times I have acted from fear have always been a mistake. Caution is one thing, fear quite another. We must move from a position of strength. Let us give our people a choice. Some should move on towards the mountain. I will go to the Gathering Place."

The three of them made the announcement.

Only four people decided to go on to the Mountain. They were all sick or injured. Seven others chose to accompany them. Some of the sick people couldn't walk well and might not finish the trek alive. Two were being carried on a sort of stretcher fashioned from poles and hides.

So, the majority of the people turned around and headed back to where the trail split. At least they wouldn't have to find the trail or clear it. The passage of all the warriors and hunters would made it easier for them. They made good time to the place where the trails merged, but it was dawn when they got there. With all the children and elders, they decided to stay there and camp.

Hypatia felt anxious and had a difficult time falling asleep.

She dreamt of battles, like scenes she'd watched in movies. She was in the middle of one of them, with a huge sword that she could barely lift. And the enemy, dressed in shabby gray-black clothing and armor was bearing down on her.

She woke when the sun had passed its high point. Unable to sleep more, she got up and paced around the perimeter of the camp, so as not to wake those who still slept. Raven joined her.

"Are we right? To interrupt the battle?"

"Death comes to all of us, but perhaps it is best to let nature decide when that time is."

His response didn't stop her fear and anxiety threaten to make last night's dried meat come back up.

At this camp, near a stream, the woodlands bustled with activity. Birds flew everywhere getting on with their lives. Singing, squeaking and cawing at each other, their bright flashes of reds, yellows and blues startling her as they streaked between trees. There were other, smaller animals she caught glimpses of, climbing through the trees. Small cat-like creatures called attas. They were the size of squirrels with gray and brown patchy fur that looked like camouflage. And she saw little sleek brown animals that stank to high heaven slithering around branches, lying in wait for birds. They were mouwlies and they smelled like rancid oil, except worse.

She tried to concentrate on her surroundings. To breathe it all in and forget about what they were going to do today. Her attempt didn't work.

Finally, she went back into camp, got her bow and quiver of arrows and found a downed log to shoot at.

By the time Hypatia finished, she felt as if some of her anxiety had lessened to a dull roar. Raven sat in a nearby tree laughing at her and trying to make her miss the target.

"Some help you are."

"If you're shooting at a real target, like today, you'll have plenty of distraction."

She gave him a dirty look, knowing he was right.

Returning to the camp, she saw people getting up, eating and bundling up their belongings. She ate a couple of pieces of dried fish and some tart berries Solia handed her. By the time she finished, everyone looked ready.

The hunters took the lead. Two of them had left earlier, about the time Hypatia woke.

The sun hadn't set yet, but was heading that way. The light in the woods was dim from all the trees. The deciduous trees were beginning to color up with pale yellow, gold, scarlet red, deep purple and flaming orange. Only a few leaves had dropped to the ground, but they created a sweet note that mingled with the predominant damp earth smell.

The forest looked stunning as they moved through it. Strange seed heads popped when touched, others hung from branches in gaudy colors, inviting birds or small animals to eat them and carry them to a new home. The smell of damp earth and moss made her feel at home. Ferns dotted the ground and large beetles scurried out of the way as people walked by.

All this beauty. Surely it could be shared by everyone.

A few hours later, the two hunters returned. The Gathering Place wasn't much farther.

Karrel's camp were already there. Most of the people were sleeping. Completely drunk, a few running races or wrestling. There was no sign of the Day People that they could see. But they might be already sleeping.

And what had Karrel been thinking? That all the other camps wouldn't figure out the elders had been murdered? That there wouldn't be repercussions?

They continued on and Hypatia's gut roiled with hunger and anxiety.

They had no plan. No way to make this work out.

They made their way down the trail finding the spot where their warriors and hunters had split into smaller groups and gone into the woods behind the Day People.

Tialla chose to follow the old trail straight into the meadow of the Gathering Place. It took some work to move through it, because it too was overgrown. Head high bushes and waist tall dried grasses with scratchy seed heads.

By the time they reached the meadow, several Day People were fighting with Karrel and his warriors. Women and children huddled close to the fire.

Karrel's movements were sloppy. He stumbled about. Thrusting and slashing with his sword. His warriors were no better. They were clearly drunk.

Tialla's power reached out to all the elders. They formed a circle. Grounding themselves and sharing their energy. Channeling it to her.

Tialla raised her arm. Light flashed across the sky like lightening. The resulting booms and screeching brought the fight to a halt. The sounds made Hypatia want to cover her ears.

"Stop!" Tialla yelled, her voice echoing through the enclosed meadow.

Then they entered the center of the grassland.

Out of the woods flooded Moon People. Warriors and hunters. Driving a few Day People.

Three Day People lay on the ground, bleeding or dead, along with Karrel and seven of his warriors. Only four of Karrel's men remained standing.

"This battle shall not continue," said Tialla with a raised voice.

A commotion came from the other side of the crowd. From beyond the hunters and warriors.

They parted and in came twenty Day People, men and women.

They looked tired and afraid. As if they'd traveled a long ways, in a hurry.

One man in front bowed at Tialla and said, "These men have attacked your people without our permission. We apologize for their actions."

One of the Day People, from the woods, spat and said, "Elias, you have no right to be here."

The first man, who must be Elias, stared him in the eyes and said, "We have every right. We live on this land too, Dar. It must be shared. It's a big land, large enough for all of us. It is you who do not have the right to make decisions for all of us. Neither did Mase," he said, pointing to one of the downed men.

The man named Dar sucked in his face like he'd swallowed a lemon.

Elias turned back to Tialla, who stood watching him. Suspicion covering her face.

"I am sorry for their actions. I have heard that they confronted you in the spring, on your way to the sea. They told you that you were no longer welcome to trade with them. They did not speak for all of us," he said, turning to look at two of the women behind them.

The women stepped forward, looking timid. They reminded Hypatia of herself, before she came to this world.

The older one, with skin browned from the sun, said, "I value the herbs and berries you bring us. I am a healer and I depend on your herbs to keep people well and alive."

The younger one said, "I too am a healer. My mother died from the wasting disease when I was a child. I wish the village healer had known how to use your herbs. My mother might still be alive."

A tall, bulky man with rough looking hands came forward and said, "I value the fresh meat and hides you bring us. I trade the hides with others as well as the meat, which I cut up into useable sizes. It helps us get through the winters."

Most of the people who came with Elias spoke about how the Moon People's trade goods had helped them.

Elias finished by saying, "I propose we build a covered area in the center of every village. In it we will leave those things you say you need. And you can come get them. In return, you can leave what we need. There need be no more of your breaking into shops to get what you need. We will give it freely. If you come at dusk, before we sleep, that will give our peoples a chance to mingle and talk. I think that would be a good thing. We each have things to share with the other."

Tialla bowed at him and turned to the other elders, whom Sanale had joined. Hypatia noticed he was grinning.

Tialla turned and looked at each of the elders in turn.

Deeorra said, "I am relieved. This is a good solution."

Solia said, "It will give us a chance to tell them how to use the herbs."

Quinna said, "I want to learn some of their stories."

Sanale said, "I would prefer peace."

Hypatia asked Raven, silently, "What do you think of this?"

"You must make up your own mind. I have food to look for," he said, flying off towards the cook fire Karrel's people had made so he could scavenge some of their roasted meat.

She'd already made up her mind. He was teasing her.

Hypatia added to the comments, "I think we have a lot to learn from each other. Peace is always preferable."

She could feel the energy streaming through the air as the other elders spoke to their individual camps what they thought about the proposal. Only a few were wary, suspecting a trap or not wanting to be that close with the Day People.

When there was silence again, Tialla turned back to Elias and said, "It is decided. We accept your offer. We wish peace between our peoples. Come, we have all travelled long and hard. Let us tend to our wounded, burn our dead and release their souls. Then we shall feast and celebrate our agreement."

Hypatia watched in amazement as downed wood was brought out of the forest and bodies were placed on it, both Moon and Day People. Nine dead all together. The fire was lit.

Only one of Karrel's men survived and one of the Day People. Karrel's camp had been the hardest hit by the tsunami. It was decided that the surviving man, women and children of that camp would be folded into Tialla's. She sent to Hypatia that they would need close watching for a few seasons.

Hypatia wasn't sure that just watching them would be enough. They had murdered or watched the murder of old people in their sleep. For power. What if the death of Karrel, the instigator wasn't enough to make them rethink his opinions?

People went into the edges of the forest, mostly the hunters and warriors, to gather downed wood. Hypatia didn't want to think about all the dead bodies in there.

A large platform was built of crisscrossing logs. When it was about thigh high, the bodies were put on it. Then it was lit, just as the sunlight topped the trees spilling down and fully illuminating the meadow.

Tialla gathered the elders and a large circle was made around the pyre. Behind the elders stood the rest of the Moon and Day People. The elders weren't touching hands, but Hypatia could feel the energy flow past and through the people just the same. It spun around the circle, picking up speed and rising high into the air like a cone. She could feel a sort of tension between the earth and the sky, which held the invisible cone in place.

Then high above the clearing gaseous blob like shapes floated into view. They were iridescent and as she watched, their outlines shifted slowly sort of like amoeba.

She felt a wave of awe pass around the circle. Behind them came deep sighs.

"The Soul Keepers," whispered someone behind her.

"Will they hurt us Mommy?" asked a child.

"No dearest. They keep the souls of the dead safe. Until it is time for them to return. I've only seen them once before in my whole life. What a blessed day this is."

Hypatia couldn't take her eyes off the shimmering shapes.

They seemed to be inhaling the smoke from the funeral pyres. At least no smoke seemed to pass above them. When it got to their level, the gray plume simply disappeared. After a time, the smoke from the fires dissipated, they drifted off, becoming paler the farther away they got. Then they vanished completely.

Tialla let the energy drop back into the earth, kneeling and touching the trampled meadow grass. All the other elders did as well. Hypatia copied their actions, feeling the excess energy flow through her fingers and return to the earth.

She stood and stretched her neck, which ached from looking upwards for so long.

"Well, that was unexpected," said Tialla, smiling.

"Have you ever seen them before?"

"Five times I've been gifted by their presence. I feel awestruck every time."

Hypatia walked around as if in a daze. How could something like that exist? They reminded her of jellyfish without tentacles. That lived in the sky. Or iridescent soap bubbles.

She stood and watched them, her neck aching. Finally, she lay down in the grass, still watching. The Great Ones moved upwards, growing smaller and more difficult to see. They gradually drifted across the sky and behind the trees.

The hunters went out and brought down some deer. Cook fires were built and the meat began roasting.

People had spread their furs or picked ferns or boughs to sleep on. Berries and roots were gathered, the roots stuck into the coals to roast.

The meadow was about one third filled with people. Over two hundred and fifty Moon People and about fifty Day People. What would it have been like had all the Moon People survived the tsunami?

Smoke from the cook fires blew her direction, smothering her in a gray cloud. The scent made her aware of how hungry she was. Her stomach had been rumbling for quite a while and she'd been ignoring it.

Across the meadow, she saw Elias and Tavor speaking. Tavor's head was down, he was looking at the ground. Then he met Elias' eyes and said something. Elias nodded and spoke again. Elias took him in his arms and held him. They must have known each other. She'd never asked Tavor about his time with the Day People. He must have known Elias. What a puzzle that boy was.

Tialla came up beside her, cradling a cup to tea in her hands. Hypatia caught the scent of mump berries and salla grass. Was it medicinal tea?

"How are you?" she asked the older woman.

"I am feeling very tired. Being a path on which magic travels can be exhausting. It gives me a small amount of energy in return, but uses up more. Still, I will be glad when we leave this place."

"When will that be?" asked Hypatia.

"Originally, our purpose for gathering here was to reunite our people. But since our numbers have diminished and we'll be together all winter in the Mountain, it seems pointless to stay."

"What about all the games and competitions, celebrating the end of summer?"

"I do not think this is a good place to celebrate right now. There has been so much death here. When the sun rises, the Day People will begin pulling the bodies of their dead from the woods. There will be more bodies burned and souls released. It is not a time of celebration. Or perhaps they will leave everything to nature. I do not fully understand their ways. I would like to leave this place, after we are rested, and move on to the Mountain."

Hypatia nodded.

She was eager to get back to the Mountain. She'd only been there a day or two before they'd started preparing to travel to the sea. The task of writing down all the stories called to her. She wanted to do that work. It had been put on hold for far too long. And she wanted to figure out a way to teach the children, and adults how to read and write. So they could write down their own stories. Perhaps the healers could write down what they knew, share it with the Day People. Every elder who died took with them their own special piece of the People's knowledge. She meant to make it possible for that wisdom to be kept by the people, not lost. As much as possible.

A large part of her wanting to move on included getting back to those comfy furs left behind. The nights were getting colder and freshly picked ferns and boughs didn't keep her warm at night. She'd been without furs since the tsunami. Others, who were older, ill or young children, had always been in more need when new skins became available. She only had the small chunk of fur to protect her left shoulder where Raven sat.

And the cold was taking its toll on her.

A man who'd chosen to be a server for this meal brought them plates of roasted deer meat and root vegetables and they went to their beds of ferns and boughs to sit and eat. The aroma of the meat made her mouth water.

She lifted the still hot meat to her mouth and tasted it. It was succulent and moist, the richness filled her mouth and she closed her eyes in pleasure.

Elias walked over and said, "May I join you?"

"Certainly," said Hypatia.

"You are not a Moon Person, yet you are an elder among them."

"I am not from this world. They found me when I arrived and took me in."

He looked at her strangely, as if grappling with the idea. "I was not aware there were other worlds."

"There are," she said. "So you know Tavor."

"Yes, he grew up in our village."

"Did he really murder people?"

"He set the fires. His mother and stepfather's house was the first to burn. Then Mase's and several other homes were set ablaze. His parents died and three others as well. Two more people were badly burned."

"That's awful," Hypatia said. How could the boy have done such a thing?

"I don't think he understood what would happen. He's young, and it's possible he didn't intent to kill so many people, only frighten them and destroy buildings. Although I'm sure he wanted his parents dead."

"Why?"

"They treated him terribly. His stepfather never thought of him as his child. They continually made him feel smaller and used him as their servant. Refused to tell him about his true father, refused to let him leave to go to him."

"Who is his father?"

"His mother knew, but no one else. Tavor still hasn't found him, probably won't if what I hear of that huge wave is true. Even before that, he may not have been alive still. Sometimes life is harsh. Tavor's not sorry he set the fires, but I believe he's sorry it killed or hurt others than his parents. Someday, he'll be sorry he killed them though. He's still so young."

"Yes, he is. If he hasn't found his father yet, you're right, he probably never will. He'll have to make his own life here. Although the Moon People are very accepting and readily adopt those in need."

"That is good then. You are the elder he looks up to the most, you know."

"Am I?" she said, surprised.

"Yes. It would help if you told him he needed to make his own life, based on his own actions. He is still so young and needs a lot of guidance. And looking after. I was his teacher, back in the village. I did what I could to help him. It wasn't enough, obviously," said Elias, looking down.

"You cannot blame yourself. If his parents abused him, then they are mostly to blame. But it's one thing to want to kill your parents, it's quite another to actually carry it out. This will be his work, to wrestle with that and somehow pay for it."

"You are right. Is everyone in your world so wise?" he asked.

"In my world there are only a handful of people who are truly wise. I am not one of those. It was only when I came here and lived among the elders of the Moon People that I truly began to see wisdom. I still have so much to learn."

"So do we all. That's why we're still here. Learning."

She nodded.

"I wonder, I've always been fascinated by the Moon People. Would I be welcome if I came to live with them for a time?"

"I believe you would." She pointed to Tialla, who was laughing uproariously at something Deeorra had said. "Tialla is the head elder. I would speak to her if I were you."

"I will do that. I would have to wait until after all the villages have calmed down a bit. Until trading has become a normal thing again. I want this transition to go smoothly. Although I think all the people opposed to it are now dead. Still, there may be some resentment and there is much grieving to do."

"Will you go into the woods and recover all the bodies?"

He sighed. "I don't have the stomach for that. I don't think anyone else here does either. No, I think we'll just let nature take care of them. We will have ceremonies for the dead in our villages, to let the people heal. But I don't think the dead will care."

"You don't think the resentment will overcome the desire for peace?" she asked.

"No, I don't think it will. I think that died with Mase."

"I surely hope so," said Hypatia. "We've seen far too much death this summer, between the tsunami and now this."

After eating, some people stayed up and talked.

Hypatia faded quickly from exhaustion. The sun had sank down below the tree tops and dusk was creeping in. She was soon asleep.

CHAPTER 22 - TAVOR

TAVOR SLEPT FAST AND DEEPLY, DEATH HAUNTED HIS DREAMS. HE woke when the night was only half over. It had been a terrible day. Slaughtering the Day People as if they were insects. Drunk and sleeping Day People. Helpless.

Just like the ones in his old village.

He rose from his bed of scratchy boughs and went to the stream to wash and drink some water. It tasted fresh and cold. Few people were awake. It had been a long grueling day for everyone. He went back to the camp and stood by a cook fire, stirring it and adding more wood to keep it going. There was cooked deer meat nearby. He peeled off a strip and ate it, savoring the juiciness of the fresh meat. They'd been living off fresh and dried fish too long for his taste. He hadn't had fish much in his life.

The sky was clear and the air hung heavy and still, as if waiting for something. The meadow was protected on all sides by the forest and didn't get many breezes. The night was silent, animals and birds quiet. The only sound was the crackling of the fires.

The arrival of the Soul Keepers had shocked him. He'd never imagined those old tales were true. Did they keep the souls of the people he'd killed in the village? Their deaths made him feel shame. It was a heavy weight to carry around.

Elias told him that somehow, he must atone for those deaths. Tavor had no idea how to do that. And now he carried the deaths of the Day People he'd killed in the woods. He knew it was different, that had been war. But it didn't feel different. He'd seen their faces, heard them cry out, felt their sticky blood. It wasn't like the fires in his village, which he'd just lit and run, never seeing the result.

He fed the cook fires for a while before one of the cooks came to him and thanked him, then took over.

He wandered off down one of the large trails that left the meadow, but didn't enter into the woods. He wanted to leave this place. To go to the winter camp. Tonight.

But he knew they'd stay at least another night. The elders were exhausted from their journey.

He decided to speak to Hypatia about his shame. And to Elias again.

He needed somehow to be released from it. If there was a way. He needed to face it, even though his first instinct was to run away.

That, he knew, was pointless.

CHAPTER 23 - HYPATIA

HYPATIA SLEPT THROUGH THE NIGHT AND MOST OF THE NEXT day. She woke when dusk was falling again. Her stomach growled and her mouth felt like cotton.

She smelled meat cooking on the fire and got up. Someone had brewed an herbal tea and she poured it into a wooden cup and drank it. It was still hot and tasted of flowers. She couldn't tell which kind. Her cup had been lost in the tsunami, but people who could were busily carving new ones. Until there were enough, people shared.

Most people were awake. Although a few had been awake a long time and gone back to sleep. Tialla looked bright and perky in comparison to when Hypatia had seen her last.

"We leave tonight," she said. "I think most everyone is ready to move on to the winter camp."

Hypatia nodded. The only reason she'd been comfortable staying this long was that this place now held for her the magic of seeing the Soul Keepers.

They ate and said goodbye to the Day People. Packed up their few belongings and left. They went down the path by which they'd come and then at the crossroads took the trail that Tialla, Hypatia and the others had gone on for a short while.

Raven caught up with her and landed on her shoulder.

"Where is your home?" she asked him.

"I travel. I haven't every really had a home."

"Have you had other people you've spoken to, helped, like me?" she asked.

"No. You are the only person I've been called to help. You were so lost."

"Called by whom?"

"Called by the air that surrounds us. The wind whispers to me. Doesn't it speak with you as well?" he asked.

"No."

"Well we ravens are creatures of the air. Perhaps the earth or the water or the fire talks to you."

"You are the only one who talks to me like this. And the other elders," she said.

He cocked his head and stared at her. "Perhaps you should speak to Tialla about this. People are puzzling to me."

He was silent after that.

They walked until the sun rose. By that time, they'd reached a break in the woods. There was a stretch of flat plains between them and the next patch of woods, out of which the Mountain rose.

"Two nights away," said Quinna.

People stood staring at it, smiling, as if seeing an old friend after a long absence.

They settled in for the day. Hypatia found a nice large bunch of sweet smelling ferns and broke off their fronds for a bed.

By the time she returned the food had been unpacked and

laid out. She took a few strips of the dried deer meat, some berries and sat down to eat.

What had Raven meant about the air talking to him? When she'd joined the others and tried to do water magic she'd felt connected to the sea. But it's not as if it talked to her.

Tialla came and sat down next to her. They ate in silence as the camp buzzed around them, filled with excitement at being so close to home.

The deer meat had been cooked and quickly dried over the cook fires of the meadow. It was rubbery and smoky tasting, but a welcome relief from dried fish. She also had a few round, dark purple berries that someone had picked. They were sweet and fruity and tasted like blackberries to her, but the texture was smooth, not lumpy like blackberries.

When she'd finished eating, she gazed off towards the plains and the horizon. She hadn't seen such a view since spring.

It was beautiful. The tall dried grasses of the plains often hid herds of striped deer-like creatures, whose name she couldn't remember.

The sun glinted off the prairie, showing that the golden color was just one of many. There were grasses colored like dusty rose, other plants a pale purple color. The color variations were a study of subtlety. One had to be looking at them.

The plains contained a beauty that wasn't as obvious as the deep greens of shadowy mossy woodlands, but it was stunning all the same. The starkness, the exposure to the elements and predators.

It was hard to survive here.

Tialla had finished eating when Hypatia remembered her question.

"Raven told me he speaks to the air and it speaks back. He

was surprised that I couldn't. He said perhaps I speak to the earth or fire or water. What did he mean?"

Tialla stared at her, examining her face thoroughly. The gaze made Hypatia uncomfortable. She looked away.

Tialla said, "Raven is a alone. Without the chatter of others of his kind to distract him. We Moon People have a more difficult time listening to wind, water, earth and fire. Some of us are better than others at it, but we all have the ability. With some, we need help hearing what is needed and how we can help. You have the ability, you can hear Raven and you can hear the other elders. I can help you learn to listen, if you wish."

"Yes, of course I want to."

"Good. Once we have reached the Mountain and I have rested a night or two, then we will begin. It's part of who we are. Being unable to hear, to make that connection is like walking around with a fur over your eyes, or over your ears. Or eating while plugging your nose. It is an emptiness which once filled, you look back on and wonder how you survived."

Hypatia nodded.

"So the people you came from are unfamiliar with the ability to listen like this?" asked Tialla.

"Yes, for the most part."

"How sad and empty they must feel."

"I think that's true. Many of them are."

Hypatia slept then, weary from traveling.

The next night was taken up moving across the plains. It had looked like such a short distance. Yet when the sun rose the next morning, they had just reached the forest. They camped inside the forest that day. Away from the blazing sun.

That night after eating they moved off on a trail into the forest. Hypatia realized that this forest was far different than the one between the sea and the Gathering Place. It was drier.

There were more evergreens and fewer trees that lost their leaves. About the same amount of moss, but she saw no ferns. Many of the evergreens were spiky and she was pleased they wouldn't be camping out. Next time she slept it would be inside the Mountain. Perhaps in her own chamber, but certainly a fur or two could be found for her.

They ran into a wide stream alongside the trail and everyone filled their water skins. The water was cold and sweet. She'd been sweating and splashed a little of the water on her face, feeling it drip down her neck. Her long hair was tied back in a leather thong, but it was still hot. Perhaps tonight, in the river beneath the mountain, she'd get a bath.

That night's journey was uneventful. Tiring, but everyone was exited about almost being at the Mountain. The last part of it was a rough climb. When they'd left in the spring she hadn't been aware of going downhill. But on the return, the opposite was obvious. The sun was long up by the time she reached the mouth of the Mountain. There were masses of people behind her.

Half a year of dust had settled everywhere and all the people coming in had stirred it up. She sneezed several times. Glow stones were handed out and she took one. She found that her memory held and she was able to find the way to her tiny little cave. There hung her backpack with all her belongings and the extra furs. She thought for a moment about taking them outside and shaking them. But didn't have the energy.

She put her bundle down on a shelf. And put her stone out into the hallway to light the way for others. Then spread the furs on the largest shelf and climbed in among them. Her stomach rumbled, but she didn't care. All she wanted to do was sleep.

Hypatia slept all that day, the following night and well into the next day. When she finally got up, warm, hungry and very thirsty, she dressed in a clean tunic and walked towards the dining hall. The large, high ceilinged cave was nearly empty.

The sun was still up. Most people hadn't gotten up yet. On one side sat the cook fires. The walls funneled the smoke upwards and out a hole near the ceiling of the large cave. Wooden tables and benches made of logs spread out over most of the floor.

Hypatia went to a table near the cook fires. She poured hot tea and dished up a plate of cooked root vegetables and some sort of meat from the previous night's dinner.

Two of the cooks were working on breakfast for tonight, chopping fruit with short knives. Periodically one would stop and go stir a huge old metal pot that hung on a metal rod over the fire. The pot looked like it had been gotten from the Day People. The thud of the spoon against the pot told her that whatever they were making was thick. The two women waved at her and she waved back, vaguely recognized them from Deeorra's camp.

She sat down at one of the long tables and sighed. As she sipped the sweet, dark tea her mind and body began to wake.

She was home again. For the next season at least. Hopefully, she wouldn't be traveling again soon. It was time to concentrate on writing down more stories. And teaching the children to write. She'd been so busy lately, there hadn't even been time to ask Casia how much reed paper had been made and brought with them. Or lost in the tsunami.

She needed to do that tonight.

Tavor entered the cave and dished up some food. He brought his plate over.

"Can I speak with you Hypatia?"

"Yes, of course."

"Elias told me I should."

"What's bothering you?"

"Ever since I came to the Moon People, I've been searching for my father. And I've asked around in all five camps and there's no sign of him. Or if there is, he doesn't want to claim me. I don't even know his name."

"Have you considered that he might be dead?"

"Yes. I have."

"The Moon People, especially hunters and warriors, don't live terribly long lives. There are many things that could have happened to him. Especially if he was traveling alone. Which he may have been, that's possibly how he met your mother."

"I know. But I've been hoping ever since I was a child, that meeting him would tell me who I am. Who I could be," he said.

She stared at him. A dangerous boy on his way to becoming a man. A lost boy.

Hypatia said, "I believe you've been given a gift. In my world, people are pretty much stuck with their parents, but as they near adulthood, they can choose what we call a mentor. Someone wise and helpful who can help them become who they want to be. I think you should spend some time looking at the people surrounding you. See who has qualities and strengths you admire. Befriend that person and learn from them. I believe that you can be most anything you want to be. You don't have to be who your parents were. I believe you make your own life."

As Hypatia sipped her tea, it came to her that's what she'd done.

This world had given her no choice but to change. And for the first time in her life, she had embraced that change and become a different person.

She felt happy.

Not just safe and secure. Actually happy. She had a home and friends. And work which she enjoyed.

Tavor ate in silence for a few minutes. When his plate was empty he stared at her.

"I think I'll always carry guilt about those I murdered. Both in my village and those in the woods near the Gathering Place. I feel like I need to do something to make up for those deaths. I don't know what that would be."

"I don't know either. That's a heavy burden to bear. I think it will take you some time to answer that question. Perhaps Elias can help you. He said he'd like to come visit and spend some time here. Or maybe Sanale. There must be something that warriors and hunters do to help them with all the death they cause," she said.

He nodded. "I hadn't thought to speak to Sanale. Or seek out other warriors. But I'll do that. And I hope Elias comes. He's a very wise man."

"Take some time to come up with a good solution. Don't rush into an answer. What's more important is that you learn from what you feel are mistakes and don't make them again. And take charge of who you want to become."

He nodded and said, "I need to go to the practice grounds. And then just before dusk Tialla said that she's meeting both of us. At the mouth of the Mountain. 'To teach us how to listen,' she said."

"Oh, thanks for telling me. I've been sleeping ever since we got here."

After finishing her food, Hypatia wandered inside the mountain, reacquainting herself with it. She only got lost twice. When there were a great many people moving about, she decided it must be close to dusk and went to the mouth of the Mountain.

She managed to find the way down to the river beneath, and bathed in the cool water.

At dusk, she found Raven outside the Mountain sitting on a

rock, catching the last rays of sun. The woods smelled refreshing, scents from the oily smelling evergreens and the loamy, damp soil.

"What will you do during the winter my friend?" she asked him.

"I will sit high in the evergreens and stay dry," he said. "And eat and sleep. Talk to other birds and sip rain off the branches. It's what I always do, winter or summer."

"I won't be outside much. I'll miss you."

"You'll be busy. You've got a lot to do."

"That I have."

Their conversation was interrupted by the appearance of Tialla and Tavor.

"Come," Tialla said, walking down a path away from the Mountain. It led deep into the forest. There was little undergrowth here. The tall trees shut out most of the moons' light. The downed logs and large boulders were covered with soft lime green moss.

Tialla perched on a boulder and said, "Sit."

Hypatia sat on a smallish boulder and Raven flew off through the trees.

Tavor took a place on a more recently fallen log which hadn't been covered with moss yet.

They both looked at Tialla. She sat with her eyes closed. Silent and breathing deeply.

"You are both older than those who normally begin this training, so I must start differently. Adults have barriers that children do not. Close your eyes and listen, feel and smell," said Tialla.

Hypatia closed her eyes. She felt the hard boulder beneath her, pressing against her folded legs. She caught the scent of the deep humus rich soil. At first the forest was silent, but then birds began to squawk and screech, warning others of the presence of people.

The breeze changed directions and she caught the scent of a muskmet, its sharp, pungent smell made her eyes water, her nose twitch and her mouth salivate. She hoped it would pass them by. Finally, it did and she could breathe more freely. One of the children had tangled with one earlier in the summer. The child smelled awful for days upon days, no mater how often she swam in the sea.

The sound of a fillenia singing made her heart lift. The tiny creatures sang beautiful melodic songs and lived high up in the trees, eating beetles and other insects.

"Now," said Tialla, "I want you to concentrate on a rock. One of the stone people. They have been here for a very long time. I want you to touch one if it helps and just sit, opening yourself to what it might have to say to you."

Hypatia put both hands on the small boulder she was sitting on. It was flat, smooth and cool. She tried to feel its energy, but there was none. It felt dead.

But no, that couldn't be right. Rock was always in the process of growing or becoming sand, then clumping up and growing again. Its life processes were just much slower than anything else around.

Get out of your head.

Stop thinking so much.

Hypatia took a deep breath and focused on her fingertips. She held them against the boulder. The smoothness felt slick and her skin warmed it.

'What do you have to tell me, friend?' she asked the stone, in her mind.

'It is time for you to be unmoving, solid, not flitting around the land. You have a choice ahead of you. Either choice is a good one. The important thing is to make it and live with it,' said the broad resonant voice in her mind.

She felt astonished that the stone spoke to her.

'What kind of choice? How do I prepare?'

'You don't have to prepare. You just have to know who you are and what you want,' the stone said.

She nodded, so bowled over by the answers that any other questions fled from her mind. She hadn't really expected a boulder to have anything useful to say to her.

After they'd finished, they went back inside the Mountain.

Tialla said, "We will meet again every dusk."

They both nodded and said, "Thank you."

The rest of the night was spent trying to hunt down Casia to find out where the reed paper was. Yes it had been safe from the tsunami. The cave Hypatia had stored it in was higher than the wave had reached. And it had been divided among four people's belongings, since there had been so much to carry.

Once Hypatia had gotten all the paper from all four people, Casia had found her again and shown her to an upper cave in the Mountain. It was a medium sized room with a large table made from logs which had been flattened on top.

"This is where I paint," said Casia. "It would be a good place for you to write and perhaps teach small groups of children."

"We wouldn't bother you?"

"Oh no. I only paint here, because it's a place I can keep all my supplies and not get in anyone's way. But the shelves for them are high and they will be safe from the children. I would like the company of others working."

Hypatia nodded.

She put the paper on a high flat shelf. With her clay pots of ink. Another person had brought all the stories she'd written down so far all the way from the summer camp. Hypatia laid them on a different shelf.

Tomorrow night, she could begin working again. Her fingers itched to write all the stories down that she'd been told on the journey to the other camps and back to the Mountain. And she also needed to write about the tsunami.

She ate dinner that morning in the great hall, surrounded by friends, Tialla, Sanale, Quinna, Casia and other. She felt at ease with them. Those from the warmer summer camps joked about the blandness of the food and the lack of spice. Those from the cooler camps declared the food perfect and that the others had lost their sense of tasting good food because they'd become used to eating too many spices.

Hypatia laughed with all of them.

The hall was full with people from all the camps. The goat meat was roasted to perfection, as were the root vegetables. Someone had been fermenting wine from berries since before they left the Mountain and it was now ready. The wine was dry, but tasted and smelled very fruity and went perfectly with the meal. She felt full and satisfied.

The next afternoon she woke early and began to walk through the woods alone. She had her bow and arrows, which she'd been told to always carry out in the forest. Raven was nowhere to be seen.

The leaves were turning brilliant colors and dropping to create a carpet of soft slipperiness; leaving trees and bushes naked, ready for winter. The farther from the Mountain she walked, the more undergrowth there was. The forest was younger here. Patches of open space appeared and the sun shone down in the larger meadows.

She stood in the middle of one, feeling the warm sun on her skin, even the air felt warm today. That would end when the winter rains came she'd been told. She'd only been here half of the Moon People's year, yet it felt like she'd lived her whole life here.

The stone's message kept running through her head.

Who was she and what did she want?

She saw a shimmering in the meadow and moved towards it. She'd never seen anything like it.

Hypatia walked around it, feeling a sort of energy coming from it.

Then she saw.

It was a doorway.

She'd been in this meadow before. It was where she arrived when she got here. Looking through the entryway, she could see the shadows of her world.

So that's what the boulder meant about a choice.

She could go back. And then she could really see how much she'd changed. She could remake her old world. Create a new life back in Seattle.

Just what she'd told Tavor he could do.

Or she could stay here and be in the life she'd created here.

'Either choice is a good one' the stone had said.

She sat down in the damp grass in front of the doorway. And closed her eyes.

Who was she and what did she want?

She ignored the sound of insects buzzing around her. Ignored the feeling of the hot sun on her skin. Ignored the fruity smell of fermenting berries on the vines.

Hypatia thought of the people here and the few she'd known in Seattle. She thought of her life here and the possibilities that could be created through that door.

Sunlight moved across the meadow, leaving her in shadow and then it went below the tops of the trees.

The doorway still glimmered at her.

Hypatia stood slowly and said, "Goodbye and thank you."

Then she turned and walked back across the meadow and into the forest.

She glanced back once and saw the door blink out of existence.

Smiling, she walked towards the mountain.

A flash of black streaked through the trees and landed on her padded shoulder.

"I'm glad you decided to stay."

"So am I, my friend. So am I."

She climbed up through the woodland towards home, a slight breeze lifting her hair.

"It's good to be home."

~

*I*f you've gotten this far, would you please consider leaving an honest review? Many readers depend on reviews to help them find their next read. It doesn't take much, just a few words on your opinion of the book. It would mean so much to me. Thank you!

ABOUT THE AUTHOR

LINDA JORDAN writes fascinating characters, visionary worlds, and imaginative fiction. She creates both long and short fiction, serious and silly. She believes in the power of healing and transformation, and many of her stories follow those themes.

In a previous lifetime, Linda coordinated the Clarion West Writers' Workshop as well as the Reading Series. She spent four years as Chair of the Board of Directors during Clarion West's formative period. She's also worked as a travel agent, a baker, and a pond plant/fish sales person, you know, the sort of things one does as a writer.

Currently, she's the Programming Director for the Writers Cooperative of the Pacific Northwest.

Linda now lives in the rainy wilds of Washington state with her husband, daughter, four cats, a cluster of Koi and an infinite number of slugs and snails.

Her other work includes:
~*Faerie Unraveled: The Bones of the Earth, Book 1*
~*Falling Into Flight*
~*Bibi's Bargain Boutique*
~*Horticultural Homicide*
All her work can be found at your favorite online bookseller.

Get a FREE ebook!
Sign up for Linda's Serendipitous Newsletter at her website:
www.LindaJordan.net
She can be found on Facebook at:
www.facebook.com/LindaJordanWriter
Metamorphosis Press website is at:
www.MetamorphosisPress.com
Goodreads: https://www.goodreads.com/author/show/
2021274.Linda_Jordan

Writers love reviews, even short, simple ones and honest
reviews help other readers find the book. Please go to where
you bought this book, or Goodreads, and leave a review. It
would be much appreciated.